BAD IDEAS\

CHEMICALS

D0508202

LLOYD

MARKHAM

PARTHIAN

'We are healthy only to the extent
that our ideas are humane.'

Kurt Vonnegut

Space Cruiser

Arms\

Orange

Spacesuit

Scabs

Through the visor of her space helmet Cassandra Fish sees the mouldy, off-white ceiling of her bathroom.

Her parents haven't come to pick her up.

As she lifts herself out of the tub, tepid bathwater sloshes on to the lime green tiles below. Unfazed, she sits on the edge of the bath and takes off her spacesuit. It is orange and although it resembles a crap film prop it can withstand long journeys through the void. Her space boots are similarly well-equipped.

Throwing her pants and bra into the laundry, Cassandra notices another blue bump like a small burrowing creature emerging from the sparse blonde grass on her thigh. This brings the total count of scratches, cuts, and bruises up to twenty-six – five more than the number of years she has been trapped on Earth. The bruises are unavoidable. The suit is not made for sleeping in. Neither is the bath. Or the boots. But these have to be endured if she is to get back home.

She eases off her helmet, wincing as hairs gummed to the inside with blood peel from her scalp. Then she lurches to the sink.

Cassandra's cheeks have sunk deeper. Her hair, which is thin and brittle, is almost down to her eyebrows and will need to be shaved soon. The planet's atmosphere is damaging her. She brushes her teeth. Then, taking a sponge and a bottle of special cleaning fluid, she sets about scrubbing the spacesuit with meticulous care.

She has a feeling that tonight will be the night her parents finally come to pick her up.

As she smooths the cleaning fluid between the fingers of her gloves, Cassandra envisions the cruiser hovering over Earth; its green lights blink, its warm engines glide towards her like gentle arms seeking to scoop, to lift, to carry—

But first a night out with her human friends.

A Bad Start\ Careers, Lifestyles & Attitudes

I am struggling to choose between three long-term career goals — killing myself, killing my dad, or killing the both of us...

Louie Jones, lying on his bed, eyes on his laptop, holds down the backspace key to obliterate the truth. Part of him wants to leave it in, if just to see his Careers, Lifestyles & Attitudes coordinator's face when she reads it. But this would only cause trouble. He mustn't cause trouble. You have to tell them what they want to hear. This is the purpose of these exercises. Envision, Articulate & Realise Training. That's what they call them. Because 'Busywork & Bullying' would make them feel bad.

Louie grimaces. Somehow a part of him still doesn't want his coordinator to feel bad. She's only doing her job after all.

He lets out a long, deep breath and starts over on his Actualisation Confessional.

I am struggling to make compromises between my long-term ambitions and my short-term needs. I have to work on my poor attitude. I have to understand that my poor attitude is why I have failed to find adequate employment...

Better. Though he will probably need to swap out 'ambition' with 'aspiration'. Ambition is something for people with means and contacts and appreciating assets. Aspiration is more appropriate, 'realistic' his CLA Coordinator would say,

5

for a young man of his class. Though she wouldn't say 'class' – that was too charged. She would say 'background'. For someone of his 'background' having ambitions was unrealistic – a bad idea. 'Ambition' suggests something forceful. Better he lays claim to aspiration – a word which rolls off the tongue in a weary gasp.

I am struggling to make compromises between breathing and...

Louie holds backspace again, destroys the black text, and rolls over onto his side – away from the laptop screen. It is eight in the morning. Soon he will have to climb downstairs and open up his father's failing shop. Louie works in this crap-hole ten hours a day but still has to claim income and underemployment support because his dad hasn't come downstairs in over a month and the angry letters from the bank are stacking up and the stock is beginning to spoil and Social Services folded their arms and will not do anything about anything about anything—

Louie feels like someone has stabbed fingers into his temples and is rooting around in his skull, scraping behind his eyes and nose.

He stands up and opens the curtains.

Rain.

Perfect, he thinks. Let it rain. May it never cease. Tip the entire ocean upon us and let the whole of Goregree sink into the sea like the stubborn, soggy log of shit that it is.

His phone buzzes. Text from the CLA:

Placement Notification. Mercy Clinic. 21:00.

He doesn't reply. Isn't necessary. Attendance is mandatory but the CLA will be thrilled if he misses the text and doesn't pitch. They can hit him with a sanction then and he will be off their books for a year at least.

Louie is only nineteen years old but he feels like a cold,

sweaty corpse. His brown hair sticks to his forehead and a blue glimmer bruise throbs as it heals in the gutter of his left eye – the result of another futile one-sided shouting match with his mad father three weeks prior.

Louie remembers going to Social Services after that incident. The taste of blood in his mouth. His heart full of grim hope that surely this time they *would* do something. How that hope so quickly crumbled as they found yet more technicalities that prevented intervention and passed him along to another sub department. He can't recall which one. Department of Excuses perhaps? Either way, it was halfway through filling the fifth form – a purple one – that something deep within him gave up and he went home, his face numb but thankfully no longer bleeding.

The last three years, since his mother had enough and left, have aged Louie a thousand fold. He feels like someone else's cursed painting – as if, in the night, some Dorian-esque twat had slipped into his room and stolen his youth away.

There is a clanking, groaning sound.

Christ, Louie thinks. Roaches in the vents again?

It is a bad start to the day.

SPACESUIT

CIDER VISOR\

TAXI BONNET

MIRACLE

Cassandra is on her way to meet her friends in town when a nearly-empty can rebounds off her forehead, splashing tepid cider down the visor of her space helmet. Through the dribble she sees a teenage human leaning by the wall of the Jones' shop, yelling something inaudible to her. She reaches into her pocket and pauses her MP3 player.

'Hey!' says the boy. 'What the fuck you wearing that for?'

Cassandra initially wonders what he is referring to but then she remembers the spacesuit. The boy, being from Earth, has likely never seen one. She picks up the can in her gloved hands, crosses the street, and places it in a bin by the shop door.

The boy eyes her up and down, fidgets with his ear piercing. 'Aw, sorry, thought you were a bloke. Bit hard to tell with that stupid getup.' He produces a cigarette from the front pocket of his red polo shirt. 'Got a light?'

Cassandra shakes her head. 'No, sorry. I don't smoke.'

'Come on now, don't be a bitch. Give us a light.'

'No, really, I don't have one.'

'Aw, be difficult then.' The boy scowls, puts the cigarette back in his pocket and storms off, disappearing into the Goregree lower housing estate.

The Jones' shop is the only general store for miles in this part of the town. Once part of a cluster of five small businesses, all four of its neighbours have since been boarded up. It now stands alone – a mass of near-identical terraced houses at its back, an impenetrable green-grey forest at its front.

Cassandra checks her mobile: 18.00. Six hours until the window of lunar transfer opens. She puts her phone away and steps through the shop door to where Louie Jones is standing behind the till nursing a head full of bad ideas.

'Er, hello, Cass,' he says, looking down at his feet.

'Hi Louie!' She points to her damp visor. 'Could I use the bathroom—?'

An unintelligible bellow sounds from the second floor.

Louie winces and turns his gaze to the gloomy stairs by the entrance of the shop.

Cassandra hasn't seen Mr Jones, Louie's father, in over a month, but evidence of his continued existence is all around the store in the faded smell of GOTE and other bad chemicals. On the wall, above the cigarettes and painkillers, a rifle is mounted on a display. In a previous life, in another country, Mr Jones had been an avid hunter. He often used to joke that the rifle was still loaded. Just in case. In case of what? Cassandra isn't sure. He had probably intended this comment as a joke. This was back when Mr Jones was still a human who told jokes.

Louie lets out a sigh. 'It's probably best if you use the staff loo.'

Cassandra nods. 'I understand. Thanks. And do you think you could call me a taxi to The Divers? I'm low on credit.'

'Sure.'

Cassandra walks to the back of the store. The chequered floor tiles are alternately clear and grimy – as if someone has repeatedly started then abandoned cleaning them. Finding the staff loo, she pushes aside the sticky door and steps into a windowless room no bigger than a cupboard with a toilet, sink and mirror rammed together like misplaced Tetris blocks. As she pulls the dangling light switch string, Cassandra hears the familiar skittering of roaches. She just about catches sight of one the size of a shoe fleeing into a vent, squeezing its black

12

reflective thorax through the loose grate.

'Roach' is the colloquial term for the species of large light-hating bugs which infest the woods of Goregree and the houses nearby. The name is inaccurate, it is unlikely they have any actual relation to the common cockroach and they look more like beetles, if anything. But once humans latch on to an idea they are loathe to let go of it. So the nickname 'roach' has stuck.

There are many stories about the insects and how they came to live in Goregree. Some say that they are a rare Amazonian breed escaped from an entomologist's collection. Others that they are an indigenous species that has been altered in a lab. No one in the town is truly certain. What is known about them is that they can grow to enormous sizes, they rarely venture beyond the woods, and, despite their fearsome appearance, they don't normally attack humans. They do, however, harm them indirectly. When the insects flap their wings, they shed thousands of tiny, poisonous, exoskeleton fragments. Over time this has polluted the air and the soil around the forest and some local people have developed a horrible illness like The Cough. Yet because the insects are essential to the production of GOTE, no one can be motivated to exterminate them.

Cassandra turns on the tap and scoops some water onto the soiled visor of her space helmet. She tries to wear her full spacesuit at all times in case she is beamed up at an unexpected moment.

Cassandra is an alien. She knows this because of a secret message coded into a film she'd seen as a child. One day her people will come to save her but in the meantime she needs to remain patient and prepared.

She wipes dry her visor with a square of toilet paper.

A knock on the door. Louie's voice:

'Taxi's here.'

'Coming now.' Cassandra steps out of the bathroom. 'Say,

13

are you coming to the Enterprise later tonight? Billy and Fox are going to be there. And Alice too I think.'

'Nah. I got a placement tonight.' Louie absently runs a finger across his bruise.

A loud honking sounds outside, along with the revving of engines.

'I better go. See you later, Louie.'

Cassandra runs out of the shop into the middle of the road only to see the taxi already rounding the corner – about to leave. Panic wells up in her gut. If she misses this ride she is going to be late for Billy's gig, late getting into the Enterprise, late getting back to her house. She'll miss the Lunar Window. She'll never get home.

The taxi reverses towards her rapidly.

Very rapidly.

She tries to move out of the way but it is as if her legs are cemented to the road.

Thump.

Cassandra rolls over the back of the vehicle, over the roof, over the bonnet.

Another thump.

When she opens her eyes she is on her back looking at the grey-blue Goregree sky. She inspects her hands, arms, cheeks, feet, chest, hips, shoulders.

Intact. As far she can tell.

Stunned, she sits up and looks around. The taxi has come to a halt a few feet down the road. Its driver is on his knees next to her, holding her hand, skin pale, eyes wide satellite dishes.

'Fucking hell, woman, are you okay?' he says, trembling.

Cassandra considers the question for a moment.

'My bum hurts,' she concludes.

He adjusts his baseball cap, then says, 'I should drive you to the hospital.'

'No. No, that's fine. Please don't.'

14

'You sure? No broken bones?'

She nods.

'Woman, that is so fucked up. It's a message. It's a message! You're, like, blessed or something! At the speed I was driving a scrawny little thing like you should have just been, like, splat!' He does a motion with his hands to illustrate. 'But, shit, I am so sorry. What can I do to make it up to you?'

'Could you drive me to The Divers pub down by Orchard Street?'

'Sure I could. It's the least I could do for running your ass over.'

As Cassandra climbs into the taxi, her nostrils are greeted by the warm, musty smell of GOTE and other bad chemicals emanating from an ornate pipe on the dashboard. Carved into the shape of a naked human woman, it has one eye and a singular, massive, drooping breast.

'Could you pass me that?' asks the driver.

Cassandra complies, shifting uncomfortably as the passenger seat wobbles and slides beneath her bruised backside. The seat has clearly been wrenched out at some point and never properly fastened back in. The carpeting has peeled off the floor and the rear view mirror is cracked. From it, a collection of knick-knacks hang from a string. Fuzzy dice. A playing card with another naked woman on it – this one with the typical number of breasts. A keyring which asserts that 'God Made Grass'.

The taxi driver widens a coffee-stained grin and pops the pipe between his teeth. 'Suppose we better get going then,' he says and starts the ignition.

The car lurches and splutters for a moment but is soon moving at a respectable clip down the narrow road snaking around the edge of the forest into the town centre. Out of the window, in the murk of early evening, amid the mass of green-grey tree trunks, Cassandra sees the yellow eyes of the roaches – sees the light of the rising moon shimmering off their shelled backs.

'I tell you,' says the driver, 'that was some insane stuff back there. I mean, thank Jesus you're okay. I tell you that motherfucker's put me through trials from time to time but he was on my side today.'

Cassandra looks through a gap in the clouds to the sky beyond and thinks about the journey she will make later – when the moon is full and lunar resonance is at its peak and the scanners of passing spaceships will penetrate much deeper into the Earth's atmosphere than normal. She thinks about those invisible alien sine-waves passing through her, enveloping her, acknowledging her. She is sure it will be tonight. This time it will happen. She just needs to get home in time. Synchronise everything perfectly.

'You're probably wondering about the accent?' says the driver. 'I've lived in Goregree a couple of years, but I ain't from around here. I'm from the States. I was a baseball player. Best damn game in the universe, I tell you. But yeah, I needed a break from all that. Thought I might come to the UK for some peace and quiet. That was a dumb idea. You from around here?'

'No,' she replies.

'Yeah, that's what they all say. No one seems to be from around here. Haven't encountered a single, genuine Goregree native. But I suppose it is a fake town. To be expected I guess.'

Cassandra gathers he is alluding to the popular local story about the founding of Goregree. The story goes something like this:

Once upon a time a rich and powerful man had a bad idea. The man's name was Dean Fritz and he was descended from a long line of successful business-humans. In his youth, in Kentucky, he'd worked as a stockbroker and hedge fund manager –

16

growing the already sizeable fortune he'd inherited through a series of ruthless hostile takeovers. However, as he entered his forties, he began to feel doubts about his life. 'I have come to believe that I am a lesser man than my grandfather,' he said once in an interview. 'Men like my grandad made a killing building bridges, trains, houses and factories, while I've made a killing tearing all those things down. I am certain that he looks down on me from Heaven with contempt.'

His peers in the business world tried to cure him of these thoughts. They told him that he was a greater man than his grandfather. That making money by building things was unreliable and risky – an archaic, primitive business best left to Asians, Africans, South Americans, etc. Conversely, making money by destroying things was sophisticated, modern, new economy. He was making the world a better, more efficient place.

But these words did not kill the ideas that were already germinating in Dean Fritz like the seeds of some parasitic flower. As the years wore on these ideas increasingly began to express themselves through what Dean called 'side projects'. This culminated in the building of Goregree – a model town constructed around a technologically advanced power plant, a self-sufficient town that would produce its own food, goods and services, a town that would exemplify the ageing Fritz's highest ideals of freedom, individualism, self-reliance, productivity, exceptionalism, and modesty.

As the taxi turns the corner and leaves the woods behind, Cassandra sees in the distance the looming unfinished dome of the Goregree Power Plant.

It hangs in the sky like a sad second moon.

Soul
Walking\
Beautiful
Butch

Alice Davies wakes up hovering ten feet above her body. Scientifically she knows this is due to GOTE's tendency to fry the temporoparietal junction, causing out of body experiences and hallucinations. Spiritually, however, she can only recognise this as the sort of thing shamans and mystics do in books and films and anime. While many addicts look at this 'soul walking' as an unfortunate side-effect, Alice finds it as appealing as GOTE's primary effect – which is an extreme heightening of sensation that the labs haven't pinned down yet. Not many institutes are interested in funding research into a drug taken exclusively by junkies in a small near-abandoned town situated somewhere between the Welsh valleys and Bristol and that isn't on any maps.

Alice inspects her body.

It is breathing.

Good.

Other than that it isn't looking so great – face down in a damp ditch, jeans pulled about halfway down, pale arse mooning the sun. Along her exposed thigh there is a field of black welts – another side-effect of using GOTE. Christ-Buddha-Allah, it isn't going to be fun at all when her mind syncs up with her body and she feels the cold mud pillowed up against her cheek.

Alice feels cold mud pillowed up against her cheek.

Fuck.

She really needs to quit.

Quit GOTE. Quit drinking. Quit smoking.

Instead she has quit her job.

It is all coming back to her. Her boss at the agency, Lindsey, had called her up at 5:30 in the morning to do a shift. Alice had told her it was too short notice. That the place was too far to get to in time for opening. That she was ill-suited for an assistant chef position as she'd never cooked anything beyond what could be nuked in a microwave.

Her boss had, as always, immediately got catty. Then shouty. Then sweary. Eventually the conversation terminated with the following exchange:

'What fucking good to me are you if you can't do this shift?'

'I don't know, Lindsey? What fucking good is your job if I don't know what I'm working or if I'm working until the last possible, miserable, bloody second?'

After that Lindsey went quiet for a bit.

Then she hung up the phone.

Alice had never said the words, 'I quit' but felt they were implied strongly enough that any further discussion would be awkward and meaningless.

God. I'm such a train-wreck, Alice thinks. The work at the agency was zero-hours garbage but it was something. It kept the twats at the CLA off her case at the very least. Well except when it didn't. Sometimes if the agency didn't find her anything for a while they would call her in and make her do a 'supervised' job search. And by 'supervised' they meant 'locked in a cupboard with a decades-old laptop while some bell-end watches you through a surveillance camera and probably masturbates furiously.

Alice groans, lifts herself off the ground and pulls her jeans up. Climbing out of the ditch she sees that she is only a hundred metres from where she lives.

'For fuck's sake, Alice,' she chides herself as she staggers up the road. 'Would it have killed you to have walked just a little bit further? A little bit further and we would have slept in a lovely bed. Well, sort of lovely. A bed at least.'

At the door to her house, she is greeted by the familiar smell of wet dog and various types of animal urine.

'You look like shit,' says a croaky voice from the living room.

'How can you tell? You can't even see me from there.'

'Because you always look like shit. Daft dyke slut.' Alice's nan lets out a dull barking laugh – like a seal with a smoking habit.

Alice sighs. Her nan is a bigot. It has taken her a while to accept this. Throughout childhood she had convinced herself that Nan was misunderstood, uninformed, from a different time. That somewhere beneath the endless flowing stream of abrasive, racist, and homophobic 'humour' there was a nice old woman who didn't really wish ill on anybody. Alice isn't certain of the exact moment this impression eroded away but she guesses it was probably sometime between the first time, when she was sixteen, her Nan had asked, 'So you have sex with women? How does that work?' and the fifty-eighth time that same year she'd asked that same question, barely containing her mean-spirited glee as she made her awkward teenage granddaughter squirm; a slug melting in salt.

'Alice, could you be a dear and go clean out Liz's house?'

'Yeah. Sure.' Alice walks into the kitchen where the lizard's cage is kept.

'Ewww.' She immediately shields her nose from the stink. The lizard is lying dead in her cage, stiff legs in the air, smelling of rot and faeces. It must have died yesterday after Alice went out. Wait. Had she gone out drinking yesterday or the day before? Or the day before that even? Her phone informs her it is the eighth. This, of course, means nothing to her. Whatever. It makes no real difference. All days are the bloody same at the moment anyway.

Alice grimaces as she takes the lid off the cage. No doubt

her nan knew perfectly well the creature was dead when she sent Alice in to 'clean out Liz's house'. Her nan is a master of using that oblivious old woman card to get what she wants. I mean, the lizard is missing an eyeball – how do you not mention that?

Holding her breath, Alice reaches in to pick up the reptile. Its head begins to wriggle.

Alice yelps and withdraws her hand as a roach, about the size of a 50p coin, forces its way out through Liz's empty eye-socket, scuttles out of the cage, and disappears into a crack in the wall. Nauseated, she hoists the dead iguana by its tail, carries it outside, and dumps it into the brown bio-waste bin. Her mission complete, she walks back through the hall.

'All done, Alice?' her nan asked.

Alice can sense her sharp-toothed grin. 'All done, Nan.'

'Thank you so much, dear.'

Alice pops her head around the living room door where her nan is sitting on the sofa eating snacks and watching wrestling on a flickering Cathode-Ray TV. Or is it MMA? Alice isn't sure. All she knows is that her nan loves to watch shirtless men fighting. Perhaps she'd been a Roman emperor in another life? It would explain the casual sadism.

'Any word from Mum or Dad?' Alice asks.

'Nah. Probably in some whorehouse in Ibiza at this point.'

Alice can't summon the energy to be disappointed. Her folks had checked themselves into rehab a couple of months ago and hadn't been heard from since. It was only meant to be a two-week stay. Alice wonders if she'll end up like that. Nah – probably dead by then.

'Go upstairs and clean yourself up,' says Nan, scooping a handful of popcorn from a Tupperware bowl. 'You're stinking up the place.'

Alice heads to her attic room. It is covered wall to wall in posters. Looking at them you can see how her interests have changed over the years. 11 – Britney and Disney. 15 – Marilyn Manson, Ghost in The Shell, Nirvana, Pratchett. 19 – Hitchcock, Velvet Underground, Kurosawa, Marilyn Monroe. 22 – Britney and Disney again but this time ironically. 24 – Margaret Atwood, Art Deco, Satoshi Kon. 26 – mostly just old Playboy covers.

She takes off her muddy clothes, lays on the bed and considers the great question of her life – shower or masturbation? If she is going to make it to the Enterprise on time to meet Billy and the others – and for her 'on time' means about two hours early so she can blitz a few drinks to calm her nerves; 'laying the groundwork' as she calls it – then she should probably head out in half an hour. Enough time for either a good wank or a good shower. Could always compromise with a quick wank and a quick shower, or a quick wank in the shower, but Alice is loathe to do this. She likes to do one thing and do it well.

For a few minutes she considers the pros and cons of a shower. A nice long shower would get the dirt out of her hair. But a minute washing her face and perhaps running wet hands through her hair would also do the trick. And besides, she's read an online article that, in contrast to popular belief, a bit of dirt and sweat was actually good for the skin and washing too much would leave her vulnerable to a variety of infections.

The pros and cons of masturbation are well explored and do not require further enquiry. It wins. Alice lies on the bed and closes her eyes. She envisions the Japanese professional wrestler Yamato Akane – a woman who, more than any other, epitomises Alice's sexual-aesthetic ideal of the 'beautiful butch' or 'soft butch'. Buff and tall but with an oval face and muscles that aren't overdeveloped or painful-looking. Alice imagines Akane's arms, her tattooed biceps, lifting her up off the ground, but not her as she is, an idealised her with natural honey blonde hair instead of a dye-job, tits symmetrical instead

25

of slightly lopsided, and no yellowy liver spots or black GOTE infections. She imagines Akane's big hazel eyes looking into hers. Or maybe not. Maybe they are closed. Maybe Akane is the shy sort who struggles with eye contact in such an intimate moment. Maybe she closes them immediately and moves in to kiss. A clumsy kiss that is all the more attractive because it is so inexpert, so sincere. Alice imagines running her hands through Akane's pink Hitler Youth hair, stroking her fingers along the border of the undercut. She imagines Akane's gold lip ring slowly brushing along her stomach as she moves to go down on her, feels the hairs on her leg stand on end as the cool metal tingle slides over her belly button. Alice imagines, wrapped between her legs, Akane's mousy face.

Mousy face?

No sooner does the thought enter Alice's mind than a vision comes to her. Not of beautiful, aesthetically perfect Akane's immaculate jawline, but of Cassandra Fish's glacial expression bearing down on her labia majora like an iceberg. Squat, skinny, gormless, Cassandra Fish who was as romantic as tuberculosis, erotic as light drizzle. The sort of petite, sexless, curveless, girl-woman that people frightened of sex were attracted to.

Dammit, Alice thinks. Why does Cassandra keep popping into her head when she is trying to masturbate? It would be one thing if they got along really well and there was some chemistry in the conversation department but she's known the woman for ages now and still knows next to nothing other than she was a childhood friend of Billy and Fox, wears a film-prop spacesuit, and looks to be about one bad Monday away from going full serial killer.

Hipster gender-flipped Patrick Bateman.

Alice giggles at herself and her cruel joke.

So much for that wank.

Hohlraum

Dirge

Divers\

Flamboyant

Fox Entrance

As Cassandra steps through the stone arch entrance of The Divers, a loud burst of static comes from the stage. Her friend Billy White is at a table by the altar adjusting one of his machines.

'You're a bit late,' he says, eyes still fixed on the device in front of him – a black tetrahedron with an aerial jutting from the top which he is slowly bending. He is a stocky, slightly short human with curly black hair, broad shoulders and olive skin that stands out amongst the pallid people of Goregree. He is dressed in a grey shirt and dark blue trousers. Cassandra thinks he looks like one of Earth's rain clouds. Back at their old school, one of the nicknames the other children used to call Billy was Emo Baggins.

'Yeah,' Cassandra mumbles. 'Sorry. Some stuff happened.'

She doesn't mention the incident with the taxi. Billy would insist on taking her to a hospital. And she is fine really. Just a bit achy and scraped up.

Billy is unsettled from his meditative gear-fiddling by a bellow from the back of the pub. 'Are you going to get on with it or what?'

'Nearly ready!' he squeaks, dropping a small device with wires attached to it.

'Look, Cass, could you go take a seat or something? I'm a little on edge at the moment.'

Cassandra nods, gets a drink from the bar, and takes up residence at her usual spot – a small table overlooked by a vacant-eyed plastic statue of Christ. It is another reminder that this place hasn't always been a pub. Originally it had been a church. Stories say it was built in the 80s by some evangelical order out of America – the kind that had their own shows on network TV and made a killing selling 'premium' membership packages. Apparently business wasn't good though so they cut their losses and sold the building on. People joked that only in Goregree could religion fail to sell. The building went through a number of owners after that. First a Buddhist goth lived in it. Then it became a South African themed bar. When that failed it became Australian. Then Irish. Then a French restaurant. Then an Italian. Then finally, about five years ago, it became a pub again – this time themed around early 20th century aviation – and was given the name The Divers. However, the current owner often grumbles that things aren't working out and that he'd like to sell up and move on. That is to be expected. Goregree is full of people wanting to move on.

From across what would have been the aisle, Cassandra sees the manager of the pub standing behind the bar. He is tapping his foot and looking up at the ceiling where, hanging from a cable, a quarter-sized replica of a spitfire slowly circles like a vulture. Its royal reds have long since faded. She pulls up her visor and sucks a mouthful of Corona through a thin straw.

A crackle comes from the performance area.

Billy has established his machines.

They are positioned on the table in rows like a company of tanks. Amidst the formation of mysterious polyhedrons a few recognisable objects stand out. An electric violin with a single string. A glass of water with a device clipped to the side. A beaker filled with thin metallic rods suspended over a Bunsen burner. A talking teddy bear with wires fountaining out of its chest. A rotatory telephone. A hammer. A biscuit tin.

'Uh ... yeah,' says Billy. 'I'm going to start now. Thank you for your patience. This composition is called "Hohlraum."'

He pushes a button.

For a moment nothing happens.

Then there is a low drone that seems to come up through the floor. And, as he lights the Bunsen burner, a high undulating noise accompanies it. Together they sound like nails tumbling down an escalator. He turns the rotatory on the phone and a whirring rhythm clanks to life. Then one by one, like a factory worker inspecting items on a conveyor belt, Billy goes along his table turning on his machines and adjusting their dials. As each one springs to life, a new sound joins his machine choir. Each one suggests motions, textures, images. Sand pouring. Water bubbling. The squeak of a windscreen wiper. The gurgle of a radiator. And so on.

Then he picks up the violin, plucks its string, and something resembling a melody emerges from the earthy, metallic din. It is a mournful tune which grows louder and louder, faster and faster, until it is rabid, desperate and nauseating.

As the hellish music climaxes, Cassandra closes her eyes, puts her hands on her cheeks. Her brain is being invaded by a vision, a memory – her mother lying motionless in the bath, eyes vacant like a bottle that has been emptied.

Then the music ceases.

The pub is silent.

Billy puts down the violin, picks up the hammer and strikes the biscuit tin.

It thunks.

'Thank you,' he says and immediately begins to pack up his things.

A few polite, uncertain claps patter around the room.

Then there is a sudden squawk of chair legs being scraped across a sticky floor as a man stands up at the back of the pub. 'What the fuck was that?' he says, puffing up his chest. He is a big human, with a thick neck and hair spiked with gel. Probably in his early thirties. It is hard to tell. Bad chemicals have a way of ageing a person.

As the man marches towards the performance area, Cassandra can sense all of Billy's muscles tensing even as he continues to quietly pack up his gear in his regimented, meticulous order.

'Oi!' says the man. 'Don't ignore me. What was that? You call that music? You think just because this is an open mic you can go on and do any old bollocks? We have to listen to it, you know?'

Billy looks at his feet as he loops a cable round and round and round his arm.

The man grabs the collar of his shirt. 'Fucking look at me!' he says. 'I'm talking to you.'

Cassandra bites her lip, feels her hands grip her Corona bottle.

It is at this moment that the human Fox Luton bursts into the bar, his scrawny arms pushing through the heavy doors in a flamboyant manner that makes one patron immediately collapse into laughter. In an instant, Fox bounds across the aisle on his long thin legs and puts a hand on the big man's shoulder.

'Hey, Evan!' he says, smiling, his voice warm like sunlight.

Immediately the man's aggressive posture melts. He releases Billy's collar, letting him tumble backwards. 'Foxy boy!' he says. 'Holy shit. How are you?'

'Fine, fine. Same old. What you doing? You look like you're about to kick off.'

'Yeah. This guy was taking the piss. So we're having a chat.'

'Him? Billy? Don't worry about him. He's a mate of mine.'

'Mate or no mate he was taking the piss, Foxy.'

'Ah, it probably seems that way. But yeah. Look he's ... a bit ... special. You follow?'

'Oh? *Ohhh*. I get it. I guess ... yeah no worries.' The man named Evan cranes his thick neck around and surveys the pub.

Everyone is looking at him. 'Aw, fuck. Now I've made a scene then, haven't I?'

'It's no trouble, man. These things happen.'

'Nah, nah. I feel like a right dick.' Evan pulls a crumpled ten pound note from the back of his jeans. 'I'm going to go. Caused enough of a mess here. Get yourself a drink, Fox. And maybe some pop for this guy or something.'

Billy scowls up at him from the floor.

Evan smiles back. 'Sorry about everything, little man,' he says. 'I'm sure your music will get better given practice.' And with that the big man walks out of The Divers into the streets of Goregree.

Once he is out of sight, Fox Luton snorts and lets out a high-pitched laugh which sounds like a goose choking on plastic.

'Oh laugh it up you bell-end,' says Billy, turning back to the packing of his machines.

'Don't take it so harsh. I mean, you are very special. To me at least. I see Cass is here.'

Cassandra shuffles over to join them, her space boots squishing on the stone floor.

'Okay then. Well, let's get going. Doesn't seem to be much of a show going on here.'

'You missed the show,' says Billy, placing his violin in its case then carefully lowering that case into the long black sports satchel that contains all his devices.

'Were you literally the only act on tonight?' asks Fox.

'Yeah. The open mic is not as popular as it used to be.'

'Oh,' Fox forces a sad, wistful smile. 'Well, I guess that's the way it goes then.'

'Yep,' Billy replies, zipping up his bag. 'Look, you guys can wait outside. I'm going to get my jacket.'

And with that he disappears upstairs.

Fox nods and heads for the door.

Cassandra sucks up the last of her Corona and puts it on the end of the bar.

The manager gives her a nod of acknowledgement.

Most people in Goregree know Cassandra. If not by name then usually as 'the weirdo in the spacesuit'. And even those who don't find it hard to be shocked by her appearance. It is hard to be shocked by anything in a town like Goregree.

Once outside Cassandra is immediately struck by how windy it has got. A sharp gust sends an abandoned packet of chips flopping off a windowsill onto frigid tarmac. The weather in Goregree often becomes calamitous without warning.

A coatless Fox shivers under a street lamp. His appearance has changed in the two months since Cassandra last saw him. He is dressed more laddish – a striped T-shirt with a plunging neckline, along with flash trainers. He can just about pull it off. Fox Luton can just about pull anything off. He is a human who can fit into any shape. Almost. Barely. Kind of. Only the very observant can catch on that something isn't quite right. That there is some other shape this human belongs in. As he smiles, street light shimmers off his green eyes and powder white skin. When they were teenagers, Fox had let his curly red hair grow down to his chin. Now it is short back and sides. A regimented rose bush permitted only a little bounce on top.

'You know,' he says, looking up at the pious exterior of The Divers. 'I was never too fond of this building. Don't like churches. Don't like being reminded of death and funerals when I'm trying to have a pint.'

'People get married in churches too though.'

'But what's the key words in marriage hey? 'Til death do us part. Marriage is as much about death as it is love. It's about choosing someone to die with. At least that's what I've always thought.'

Cassandra shrugs. 'I guess,' she says, staring at the moon, her mind drifting again to Alpha Centauri and her fateful

34

return home.

The door to the pub creaks open and Billy steps out in a smart black jacket, his bag slung over his shoulder.

'You look like a vampire,' says Fox. 'Well, a tanned one. Maybe like a gyppo vamp?'

'Well, you look like a cunt,' replies Billy, smiling. 'Actually, to be more precise you look like an exposed, shivering clit.'

'Christ! Steady on now. It's too early in the evening for that sort of talk. You've been spending too much time with that Alice. She's a bad influence. Filthy mouth on that one. Hasn't got a shred of human restraint.'

'Don't lecture me about influences. What the hell are you wearing? And where's your coat? This isn't Ibiza – you'll crystallise walking around like that.'

'Don't need a coat. We're going to a club. I'm not going to look like a dweeb lugging a jacket in, checking it into the cloak room. There – you see that lot?' He points to a group of broad-shouldered men and mini-skirted women further down the road. 'Not a jumper among them. They know what's up.'

'They're imbeciles.'

'They could be astrophysicists for all you know.'

'Whatever. Let's get a move on. I've got to drop my gear off at mine on the way.'

Fox nods and him and Billy set off down the road.

Cassandra follows after – near but a little apart from the two human boys.

Together the three of them move down the road in a little 'T' formation not dissimilar from how they had marched down the school hallways when they were teens. Back then their little group was known by a few names. The nicest of these was the Orphan Three. Typically though they were called nastier things – the Emo Orphans, the Gay Orphans, the Goth Orphans, the Orphan Fags. And so on. There was a running theme.

Cassandra still doesn't understand these names. For one thing, only Fox is an orphan. Billy's father was taken by The Cough, but his mother is very much alive. And neither of Cassandra's parents are dead – both her mother and father returned to Alpha Centauri through the Lunar Window. And 'Emo' is similarly erroneous, because, while Billy and Fox could certainly be overly emotional, Cassandra reckons she is very rational. As for 'gay' – well that is a more nebulous issue. Cassandra has always been disinterested in sex with humans of any sort, but with the boys it is more ambiguous. She knows that Billy had sex with a female human once but it was hard to tell if he really enjoyed it and from what she has seen he hasn't sought to repeat the experience. Fox's escapades are similarly mysterious. He jokingly flirts with men and women all the time but never appears to go further than that. Neither of them openly express a preference.

Cassandra's space boots thud on the sidewalk. The stillness and emptiness of Goregree's streets make her footfalls seem unnaturally loud. All around, deserted buildings lie in rows like graves. Tombstone signs mark them: For Sale. Closing Down. Everything Must Go. They are on Market Street – the abandoned, silent part of Goregree. As you get closer to Market Street, buildings die one by one until all that is left are these haunted grey hulks.

Goregree. Gooor-greeee. The name feels unnatural coming out of Cassandra's mouth. She'd heard it was just some made-up nonsense Dean Fritz, the founder of the town, had cooked up – two syllables he'd thrown together because they sounded, in his words, 'like some old kind of British' in a way that was apt. Fake, made-up name for a fake, made-up town.

'So,' says Fox, breaking the quiet. 'How did the show go?'

'I'm guessing you mean before I got yelled at?'

'Yeah.'

'Hmmm.' Billy pauses, appearing to consider the question.

'It was fine.'

Cassandra is not exactly sure what measure Billy uses when determining the success of his performances. It is hard to tell if he enjoys making his music at all. It seems to pain him, but the more it pains him the more insistent on making it he becomes.

'Hey, Fox,' says Billy. 'Thanks for helping me out back there.'

'I wouldn't have needed to if you didn't go all icy. If you just cracked a joke or smiled or something he probably wouldn't have kicked off.'

'So I'm meant to be pleasant and congenial when someone I don't know shouts at me and invades my personal space?'

'No, no, you're twisting what I said. Look, I know it's shit, but it's to be expected in this town. You'll make life a lot easier for yourself if you just get used to a certain degree of low-level ambient aggression.'

'Maybe I don't want to get used to it? Maybe I can't. Maybe if I was able to I'd have gotten used to it a long time ago. We're not in school anymore.'

'You see, this sort of attitude is what sets people like Evan off. You radiate angst and people like him, they take it badly. They think you're putting on airs. They think you're directing it at them. If you reined it in, even just a little, they'd warm up to you. And they're not such bad guys. I mean, Evan is a complete puppy dog once you get past that tough squaddy exterior. You've just got to be sensitive to their feelings.'

'I have to be sensitive to their feelings? Why? Why can't they be sensitive to my feelings?'

'You can't make friends with that kind of attitude, Billy.'

'I don't want to be friends with them. That's what you don't get, Fox. I just want them to leave me the fuck alone. But they never will – no matter how old I get, the fucking Evans of this world always hunt me down. And now you're dressing like one.

It's nauseating.'

The Orphan Three reach the narrow cul-de-sac of terraced houses where Billy lives. Tomorrow is garbage day and black bin bags are by every gate. No one knows who exactly collects them. Apparently, being a fake town built on a remote spot along the border between England and Wales, there has long been disagreement over whose exact jurisdiction Goregree falls under. But, mysteriously, the garbage always gets collected and from time to time the lights in the old council building flicker on and there are some rudimentary social services running. Perhaps some old agents of the Fritz estate still perform basic duties for the place?

There is a rusty squeak as Billy pushes past the gate to his house and walks inside. Although Cassandra has been to his home many times she can never quite remember which one on the street it is. They are all doll-house-white squares of concrete, indistinguishable from one another. A few minutes later, Billy emerges with a red tracksuit top slung over his shoulder. He locks his front door, stomps down the pebbled path, and shoves the jacket into Fox's hands.

'Before you freeze,' he says.

Fox lets out his goose-giggle. 'Usually someone has to buy me a drink before I'll play dress up with them.'

'Haha. Just put it on. I can't stand to see you shivering your nipples off. Twat.'

Fox smiles. 'Okay then,' he says, slipping on the tracksuit top. It has white trim along the collar and sleeves and the red matches his hair perfectly.

Cassandra smiles. Billy is good at picking out clothes for people.

'Great. Let's go then. Enterprise is only going to get busier and I'll be fucked if we're standing the whole night.' He walks on ahead, his black hair fluttering in the wind. Fox follows after, beaming as he inspects his new coat. Cassandra checks her mobile: 20:30. She feels a bristle of excitement.

In less than four hours the Lunar Window will open.

GREY

MERCY\

"I..."

A warehouse. Whenever Louie is given a placement at the Mercy Clinic for Assisted Dying it always strikes him how much it looks like a warehouse. The only hint that the green-grey block does not contain office supplies but dead and dying human bodies is the fraying poster by the door which depicts a man knelt by an elderly woman in bed. Beneath these figures a slogan in blocky art deco font reads, 'The Greatest Duty of The Young Is To Help The Old Pass On'. It is an old advertisement from when Mercy first cropped up – around the time the government privatised the NHS euthanasia services and relaxed the regulations around palliative care, mental health treatment, and assisted dying. Mercy's unique selling point is the idea that young people on benefits should provide comfort and assistance to the more elderly who had decided to pass on but who had no relatives or friends to support them. This has the added bonus of allowing Mercy to cut nurses and rely on the CLA to provide them with a heavy rotation of temps and one-off placements.

Louie steps through the door. It closes behind him suddenly and silently as if in a hurry to move him along. Inside is a windowless reception with off-white walls and brown carpeting full of gum, grime and the occasional squashed roach.

'Can I help you?' asks the receptionist.

'Um. I'm here to do a placement.'

'Name?'

'Louie Jones.'

'Hmmm.' The receptionist puts down her knitting

needles and scowls over a register. She is a very short woman with a crown of grey hair that spins upwards like the points on a star. She ticks a box and draws in a long breath, the hairs under her nostrils wobbling like insect feelers. 'Go through to the prep room and get your uniform from Kyle.'

'Thank you.'

'You know your 'placement' used to be someone's job.' The woman spits out the word 'placement' as if it were a bit of rotten fruit, and resumes her knitting.

Louie nods and continues down the hallway to the prep room. Stepping inside, it is much the same as before – a long windowless room with lime walls and no furniture. At its far end is a counter not unlike the sort you'd see in a post office, only the glass screen is grimy, almost opaque, and circular like a submarine window. Beyond, Louie can just about make out Kyle. In the hazy glass he appears as a thin ginger moustache pasted onto a pallid oval smudge.

'Hello. I need a uniform?'

'Oh. Sure. Here you go.' Kyle slides him a blue outfit from under the screen. It can almost pass for a nurse's uniform if you don't pay close attention.

'Um, this isn't my size.'

'Sorry. New policy. One size fits all.'

'Okay.'

'Do I recognise you from somewhere?'

'The CLA have placed me here before.'

'Oh. Guess that makes sense. You remember the drill then?'

'Yeah. Go see Jen in recruitment and then go get changed?'

'Yup. No problem then.'

The smudge behind the counter falls quiet.

Clutching the crumpled uniform to his chest, Louie leaves the prep room and rounds the corner. There, at the end of the hallway, are two rooms and some stairs leading upward. One of the rooms is a staff toilet. The other is Jen's office.

He knocks on the door.

'Come in,' says a tiny voice.

Louie enters the room. It hasn't changed. Sparse yet somehow messy. A single desk on top of which a bulky grey desktop PC, a printer, and stacks of printouts, are crammed, looking like they might spill on to the floor at the slightest disturbance. A wastepaper bin overflowing with crumpled sheets, tissues and sweet packets. In the corner, a dusty model skeleton faces away as if ashamed. And, at the back of the room, towering over the desk, is a long, black cabinet.

'Oh, hello, Louie. Another placement with us?'

He takes a moment to spot Jen amidst the detritus, idly jabbing an empty syringe into an injection training model over and over again. Jen is very short and often sits so still that she blends into the scenery. Her hair runs all the way to her backside. Louie thinks she looks a bit like Cousin It or something out of a Jim Henson production. Then he thinks that he is cruel for thinking that. Then he thinks that that kind of repression – the constant second guessing and chastising of negative thoughts – is exactly why he has been a doormat his entire life. Then he thinks that that sort of comment is exactly the sort of thing his father would say when he'd had a bit too much to drink. Then he thinks again about whether he should shoot himself or his dad or—

'Hello? Earth to Louie.'

'Oh. Yes. Sorry, Jen. Away with the fairies.'

'Well, don't spend too much time with them,' she says, smiling dryly, standing up. 'Anyway, let me get you what you need.' She opens the cupboard doors. Then, standing tiptoe on her office chair, reaches for a silver zip-lock bag on the top shelf.

Jen has taken off her shoes and socks. Seeing the bare arch of her foot sends an odd twinge of desire through Louie. As he feels an erection coming on, he wonders what the hell is wrong with him.

'Here's what you need.' Jen hands him the zip-lock bag. 'Your client is on the second floor – room 205B.'

Louie nods and darts next door to the bathroom.

He exhales and feels his heart rate steady and, eventually, his erection wilts.

The staff bathroom of the Mercy Clinic is wastefully large. Inside, Louie always feels like a trick of perspective is being played on his eyes – as if he is peering into a funhouse reflection. He quickly unwraps and puts on his uniform. Reflexively he checks himself in the mirror only to remember that there isn't one. He washes his hands and face in the sink and steps out into the hallway – the silver zip-lock tucked under his arm. Then he heads up the stairs to the second floor, holding on to the railing as he does, feeling flecks of paint peel off in his palms like dried glue.

At the top, Louie finds himself at the end of a long corridor lined with numbered doors. He inspects the first one. 201A. The next, 202A. And so on. He walks down the hall and counts – 205A ... 208A ... 215A ... Just how long does he have to go until he reaches the Bs? The longer he spends in the Mercy Clinic the more he feels unsettled by it. What is with the lack of furnishings and decoration? Would it really break the budget to put up a picture? And what is it with this thick gooey carpet? The most unnerving thing, however, is the absence of any human noise. Surely there should be speaking, whispering, crying, laughing. At the very least breathing?

205B.

Louie stands for a moment, hand resting on the door handle, trying to compose himself, to summon up a smile.

Smile.

Yes.

He should at least do that.

Then he steps through into a little room. A bleak little room with a bare desk, a bed and a large window that offers only a grey view of a concrete wall. Maybe if you stick your head out and crane it up or down, left or right, you might be able to see the sky, the ground, the road, but that is a moot point because the window doesn't open out or in and is barred with iron so that no one can jump out to their non-state-approved deaths.

'Grim evening out, isn't it?'

Louie turns to see his client sat in the far corner of the room, arms cradled around her knees.

'I couldn't bear to look at it,' she continues chipperly. 'And this seems to be the only part of the room I can't see it.' She lets out a nervous laugh. The woman is younger than the other clients Louie has assisted – surely no more than sixty. She is white-haired, whisper-thin, dressed in a long polka-dot dress, and has an anchor tattooed on her right shoulder.

'Well, should we get started then?' she says, standing up then sitting on the corner of the bed, facing away from the window.

Louie sits next to her. Up close he can see that there are scars all along her wrists. He begins to wonder. Why the polka-dot dress? It looks new. Did she pick it out especially for this occasion? Why the anchor tattoo? Is it a drunken teenage dare turned heirloom? What is her background? What led her to this place?

As he opens the zip-lock bag and pulls out the syringe, Louie simultaneously feels two irreconcilable desires to at once know everything about this woman and yet also know nothing, to be wiped clean and left blank like a spotless white sheet.

'As an employee of Mercy,' Louie begins, 'I am obligated to remind you at this moment of your rights...' And so on. Without pause he emits a bureaucratic chant to ward off bad fortune, lawsuits, etc, etc. After ten minutes he reaches his legally ordained anticlimax— '... if you would like to proceed please confirm one last time. If you have any doubts then we at Mercy would urge you to reconsider, Madam.'

She forces a smile. 'Yes, please go ahead, boy.'

'Can I take that as a confirmation, Madam?'

She sighs. 'Yes.'

Louie holds up the syringe, lightly presses the plunger, and inspects closely a tiny drop of clear fluid oozing from the tip. It is working.

At the sight of the needle, the woman quickly looks away.

'Alright,' he says. 'I will begin.'

She nods, looking at her feet.

He holds on to her arm and sticks the needle in.

She flinches.

He slowly pushes down on the plunger.

She winces. Then, as the last milligram of poison enters her veins, her face un-tenses. She looks up at Louie. Her eyes are clear blue and Louie cannot imagine how he must look in them. Is he a cold, unpleasant comprehensive school cherub? A disinterested devil? Some teenage summer job ferryman?

She opens her mouth to say something.

'I...'

And that is it. Her blue eyes roll upward as if to follow her spirit's ascent. Her body goes limp and slumps toward the floor. Louie quickly catches, steadies it. He is surprised how heavy it is, given how slight she appeared. Or maybe this is normal? Maybe human bodies are heavier than he'd thought? It is so easy to forget, when you see them in motion, how much effort goes into making them move, how much strength is needed to carry them. A person might go their whole life only ever managing to carry one – their own. A person might go their whole life and not even manage that.

Louie is still holding on to his client's arm.

He has been holding on to her arm for a while now.

Maybe ten minutes. Maybe fifteen.

Sitting next to her empty body as gravity tries to pull it downwards.

The woman's arm is cold.

His hand is cold.

He wonders which had been cold first, which had frozen the other.

Standing up, he gently lays the body on the bed as neatly as he can.

Then he stands up and walks back into the hallway. He spies the black, upturned corpse of a Roomba-sized roach,

48

glistening in the dirty carpet fur like wet dog shit.

Next thing, he is in the staff bathroom, scrubbing his face in the sink with hot water, feeling his adolescent skin scabs peeling off in his fingernails, feeling his adolescent needle-prick chin hair sliding under his fingernails.

Louie doesn't remember walking downstairs or turning on the tap. His body seems to be moving and responding automatically – like he is experiencing some strange allergic reaction.

Louie thinks about his client. Was she really given a proper psychological evaluation? The Mercy Clinic, and all of the companies who work in assisted dying, are required to do thorough background checks and examinations of all persons requesting euthanasia. However, it is well known that regulation is lax and that this requirement is not rigidly or consistently enforced.

Louie thinks about her last words.

Did he hear them right? Maybe what she'd actually said was not 'I' but 'I've...'

Maybe what she was going to say was, 'I've changed my mind.'

There is a sudden, sharp pain in his shoulder. He probably pulled a muscle when he darted to catch her body.

Despite his sore shoulder and feelings of emptiness, it isn't as bad as his first placement with Mercy. That had involved an old man who, as the needle went into his arm, put his hand down into his trousers and began trying to tug one out. He didn't succeed. The poison finished before him.

I've changed my mind.

Louie wonders why he has come here? What is the point? He's already decided to end things. Perhaps he'd thought he might encounter something miraculous here, something that would reinvigorate him or at least frighten him off his present path. Instead he feels even more convinced that he is making the right decision, taking a step in the right direction.

I've changed my mind.

Louie is now outside, resting against the wall of the clinic. The night is very dark now. The lights of the clinic seem weak and small as if retreating inward into the building – waiting behind its concrete walls for the dawn.

Standing by the door, grumbling as she fidgets with a faulty e-cig, is Jen from recruitment.

'Fucking thing,' she mutters to herself, before finally getting the device to work. She breathes in, then breathes out a swell of green peppermint vapour. Then her eyes widen as she notices Louie, sunken by the wall.

'Hey? Louie? You alright?' she asks in a tone very different from how she usually speaks to him. 'It's been, like, an hour since I signed you out, what you still doing here?'

Louie opens his mouth. The words he intends to come out of it are, 'Oh, I'm just sitting here having a think. About to head off. It's no worry, Jen.'

Instead what comes out is, 'I've changed my...' followed by silence.

'You've changed?'

'No, er, sorry. I'm really out of it, Jen.'

'I can see that.' She walks right up close to him and peers up at his expression, searching it as if examining a wound.

For the first time since they'd met two months prior, Louie gets a good look at Jen's face, which is usually obscured by her hair. Her eyes are wide and bird-like and she has a little black birth mark on her left cheek bone. Louie finds her incredibly attractive. Though he wonders if that is just because the last woman he'd seen is now lying dead in the building behind them. What did they do with the bodies after? What was the procedure for removal, disposal, etc? Louie feels his temples begin to ache.

'Hmm. I get it,' says Jen, as if concluding a diagnosis. 'Tough placement?'

Louie nods.

'Tell you what – how about a smoke?'

'Huh?'

She smiles at him, revealing slightly crooked teeth. 'A smoke? Fancy one?'

'Um, I don't smoke.'

'Oh, not this,' she says, tapping the e-cig. 'I mean ... you know? GOTE.'

Louie nods.

'Okay then, follow me.'

Jen leads him round the back of the building to a grey parking lot that is empty but for a single car – a battered four-seater the colour of cigarette ash. A family-sized car that seems too large for tiny Jen and him. You can almost stand up in the thing.

'Climb in,' she says as she squeezes the electronic lock – eliciting a loud beep from the vehicle – and gets in.

Louie pulls on the handle.

Nothing happens.

'Oops,' she says. 'Forgot the passenger door is buggered. You'll have to get in on my side.'

Louie nods and goes round to the driver's seat where Jen is leaned back, puffing on her e-cig. He hovers by the door for an awkward moment before realising that she isn't getting out to let him past. He carefully clambers over her into the passenger seat. As he does this Jen looks at him with a wry smile, as if she is in on a joke unknown to him. Louie feels his breathing quicken.

Once he is settled in his seat, Jen turns on the ignition. The lights in the car come on and are dim. So dim they somehow make the brown faux leather interior seem darker, dingier. The radio squawks on. One of those classy types of late night shows is playing. The type where classical music is played and the meaning of it discussed in hushed, reverent tones. The piece playing at the moment however is neither hushed or reverent. It is mad and desperate-sounding, full of lurching violent energy – an impression amplified by swelling waves of intermittent static.

Jen fiddles with the dials.

'Sorry,' she says, 'stupid thing's reception's wonky.' After a minute of tinkering she eventually sighs, 'Stuff it,' and turns the thing off.

'Anyway,' she continues, retrieving some rollies and filters from the cubbyhole. 'There should be a bag by your feet, could you grab it?'

Louie bends down and waves his hand blindly around the floor of the car.

'No, no.' He flinches at Jen's hand on his leg. 'Not there – there. A little to your left. No. That's too far now. Back a bit.'

'Sorry. I can't see anything in this light.'

She giggles. 'Don't worry. You sit back. I'll get it.'

Jen puts down her e-cig on the dashboard, slowly climbs over onto his lap and crouches down into the dim recesses by his toes. Suddenly the car, cavernous before, feels awfully cramped.

'Oh. Actually, maybe it's by the other foot,' Jen remarks. As she squirms around looking for the GOTE her backside pushes back further and further into his crotch. If Jen has noticed or is bothered by Louie's obvious erection she gives no indication.

'Ah. Here it is,' she says.

'Can I kiss you?' Louie blurts out.

'Alright then.'

Louie turns her around to face him. Cradles her cheeks in his hands. Brings her lips an inch from his. Her eyes shut. His eyes shut.

Blood floods every vein in his body. Every vessel swells. Every organ boils red like an overheating engine. Moments crash forward, disconnected, one into the next. Jen's long hair curled in his fingers. Jen's legs in the air, wrapped over and around his shoulders. Jen's bare knees by his ears. Jen's arms around his neck. Jen's low breathy gasp.

Then it is over.

Its ending as sudden as its beginning.

They are naked from the waist down, he inside her, she

folded in half beneath him on the passenger seat – which at some point in the frantic fifteen minutes had been cranked backward.

As Louie's brain rises bewildered out of the soup of blood and heat in which it had been subsumed, he feels half-tempted to ask what on earth had just happened.

'Hey,' says Jen. 'Could you pass me my e-cig?'

Louie nods, climbs off of her, grabs the device off the dashboard, and hands it over.

'Cheers,' Jen says, dragging in green vapours. 'You like to come over mine for a bit?'

Louie thinks about it. Nods.

Before he knows it they are driving down the road away from the centre of town and deep into the suburbs. Then further still into the bad suburbs. The suburbs that are little more than textureless blocks that meld seamlessly into the roads and the side-walk and electrical poles and telephone wires until everything is an indistinguishable horizon of concrete and copper-wires.

As they traverse the length of the town, Jen, who reveals her full name to be Jennifer, talks about her favourite metal bands, how metal was so much better when she was growing up, but that she still finds the odd new band she likes.

Louie mostly just nods.

Moments are crashing disconnected, one into the next, into the next, into the next, into the—

Enterprise\

A Dream

From Alpha

Centauri

When Cassandra Fish and the boys arrive at Enterprise there is a queue. Fifteen people lined up outside discussing their minor discomforts, exchanging gossip: Did you hear about what he did ... This one time she ... I never really liked him ... She totally went down on ... Knocked up some girl I hear ... She's a weird one ... He's a prick ... It all runs together and bounces around like marbles in a playground. At times Cassandra finds she really has to focus to understand what it all means – the gobbledegook that comes out of human mouths.

This is because she is an alien.

The truth of her alien heritage had been revealed to her many, many years before by a film she'd seen. It was called *They Came from Alpha Centauri* and she'd come across it while flicking through TV channels late one evening, when her foster carer had gone to bed. It was an old-fashioned science fiction film – the title card written in a big green and purple font.

They Came from Alpha Centauri was about a group of aliens who journeyed to Earth to study humanity in secret. In order to better infiltrate human society, they took control of organic machines built and designed to look and work exactly like human bodies – empty shells for their alien minds.

For a while their plans were successful and they compiled lots of excellent reports on how humans worked. However, the longer the aliens spent on Earth, the more they became attached to their human shells. Before they realised what was going on, they became stuck. Unable to teleport back into their real bodies which were being stored on a hidden space platform orbiting the Earth. Then, slowly but surely, they forgot that they were aliens altogether.

They thought that they were humans.

They lived out human lives.

This wouldn't be such a problem for another alien species but these aliens were from Alpha Centauri. Their planet was made entirely of water. All the aliens on Alpha Centauri lived in giant underwater cities. On Alpha Centauri human methods of communicating, of socialising, were totally redundant. Everyone was telepathic. The minute someone laid eyes on you, they instantly knew how you felt, what you'd been up to, your ideas, your hopes and your dreams – everything was communicated perfectly and cleanly.

There was none of the awkwardness, the fumbling, the embarrassment, the deception. There was no need for the extrapolations and imprecise descriptions which destroy and mangle every bit of truth a human might try to convey. There was no need for arguments, or bickering, or war, because how could you lift a sword, or shout a curse against a person whose mind and pain you knew as well as your own?

Naturally, an alien born on such a gentle planet would always be at odds with a place like Earth. Deep down the Alpha Centaurians could never truly adapt to human life. They became dysfunctional and unhappy. They did their best to get by – attended therapy sessions, drank booze, took lots of bad chemicals. But they felt a constant sense of absence, of emptiness, that they could not explain and which chipped away at them daily like sea water eroding stone.

This carried on for several years until one day a spaceship from Alpha Centauri passed by Earth on a routine surveillance mission. Its sensors detected the stranded aliens and one by one they were beamed up from their human bodies.

In the final scene the lead alien scientist, a woman who looked like Cassandra's mother, lay in the bath, staring upwards as her eyes twitched and emptied of life. It was at this moment her alien mind was sucked from the human shell that imprisoned her, leaving behind an empty vessel.

While watching this scene, something clicked in Cassandra's young brain – as if a mechanism that had been lying dormant within her had begun to tick and whir and come to life. She knew from that moment on that she was from Alpha Centauri. That her mother was from Alpha Centauri. And so was her father – a man she had never met but imagined vividly.

Her foster carer at the time tried to dissuade her from this. She explained patiently that the film was a fiction. And either way Alpha Centauri was a star, not a planet.

But it was too late. The idea had already flowered within Cassandra. It had whispered to her and explained away all her aches and pains and terrible memories. Her mother and father are waiting for her on Alpha Centauri. No. In fact they are searching for her at this very moment. She knows this. It is certain.

'What's certain?'

'Huh?'

'Certain,' Billy repeats. 'You said that something was certain, Cass?'

'It's nothing. Just talking to myself.'

'Fair enough.'

They are near the front of the queue now – the club called Enterprise looms above. It is *Star Trek* themed and shaped like its TV spaceship namesake. The construction was funded by an eccentric pop star in the late sixties – a greasy man with thick sideburns who had a lot of money and a lot of bad ideas. The body of the building is held up high in the air by four large supports, which were originally painted black so that at night it would appear as if the club was hovering above the ground. It was so effective a ruse that people kept walking into them, so now they glow fluorescent yellow and are circled with warning signs and red lights.

Reaching the entrance, the Orphan Three stand before a see-through lift which has been designed to look like the transporter from the TV show and is notorious for getting jammed.

Fox smiles at the attendant who operates the device and steps inside. Billy and Cassandra follow in after. Slowly the lift croaks to life and rises.

'Fingers crossed,' murmurs Billy.

Cassandra places her hand against the glass, spreads out her orange-gloved fingers like a starfish, and looks out at the town beyond and between her digits. She recalls the time Billy got stuck in here and lost his virginity. He was seventeen and full of booze and bad chemicals. The girl sharing the lift with him looked about the same age. Cassandra didn't know if they were acquainted beforehand or who initiated the act – which lasted about twelve minutes. She observed the event from the ground below, through the lift's see-through floor, while the bouncer, who didn't care enough to complain, focused on repairing the broken mechanism. Afterwards, when she, curious about a few things, tried to speak to Billy about the incident, the teenage boy cried and said he didn't want to talk about it – a reaction she found mysterious.

Cassandra finds many of the things humans do mysterious.

There is a clank and a jolt as the lift finishes ascending. The doors open and a fizzle of green smoke billows up from the hinges like they are emerging from a cryogenic tube.

The clammy heat of the club steams up Cassandra's visor. She wipes it clear but is left with a hazy smudge of moisture through which she tries to take in her surroundings. It has been a while since she's been to Enterprise but it looks roughly the same as before. The inside is where its *Star Trek* theme falls away. The original furnishings were expensive to maintain, so over time they had been replaced with more conventional fare until nothing but the exterior hull was as the original designer intended. The lights on the ceiling are blue. The surfaces, black, synthetic, easy to clean of booze, sweat and other bodily fluids.

Cassandra feels thick fingers grip her shoulder.

She turns to see an unfamiliar bouncer's face. A new guy?

'What's with the spacesuit, love?' he asks, as Billy shoots

him a dirty look.

Cassandra takes a moment to realise what the tall man, whose head sticks out of his black suit like an egg in an egg cup, is referring to. She has been wearing the spacesuit daily for over half a decade and its presence is almost invisible to her now. It is a prop from *They Came From Alpha Centauri* that she'd bought off the internet for a big sum. Of course, she knows that it is really more than a prop. On the slim chance that her parents locate her when she isn't near an aquatic conduit, it would allow her to be beamed up. Besides, she likes the suit. When she slips it on and feels the plastic against her skin she senses she is a little closer to Alpha Centauri – to home.

'Don't worry about it, Joe,' says another bouncer. 'She's okay. Not quite all there, but okay.'

'Alright,' says Joe, letting go of Cassandra's shoulder.

The Orphan Three continue on in, skirting around the amorphous crowd by the bar.

'Cunt,' mutters Billy, once they are out of ear shot.

'He was just doing his job,' says Fox.

'Please. There was no need for him to be puffing up his chest like that. Does Cass seriously look like the sort of person who's about to kick off?'

'Oh, leave it. Let's not have another argument. Get some drinks instead. What do you want?'

'You don't have to get me anything.'

'Don't give me that. Let me get you a drink. Least I can do after you got me this lovely jacket.'

'Ah, sod it. Okay then. Pint of Guinness.'

'This is a club, Billy. You're not getting a Guinness here.'

'Oh yeah. Hmm. Alright, I'll leave it to you. You can pick a drink for me.'

'Haha. You will regret that decision, Billy White. And Cass? Vodka Martini I take it?'

'Another Corona would be nice,' says Cassandra.

Fox nods. 'Okay.' Then he disappears into the blob of humans by the bar.

Billy makes a throaty grumbling and marches off in the direction of the stairs. Cassandra follows after, her space boots squishing on the club's gummy floor. She recalls a conversation she and Billy had back in Year 11. They were at the place where they came every break time to eat, talk, and avoid other people – a small algae-covered pool circled by fallen trees.

That muggy afternoon, Fox, who was usually with them, had been sent to detention for a prank he'd done to try and make the other students like him. Fox was always trying to make people like him. Maybe it was because, unlike Cassandra, he had actually been adopted once before, but after six years his adopted parents changed their mind and Social Services had to take him back into care. Maybe that made him more desperate for acceptance than her and Billy. He always joked that, unlike Cassandra, whose parents were on Alpha Centauri, and Billy, whose mother was alive, he was a true rootless orphan.

'Billy,' she'd said, unravelling the cling film from her Marmite sandwich. 'Why do you hang out with Fox?'

'What?'

'It's just you seem to be such different humans. You irritate each other and fight all the time. Why put yourself through it?'

Billy was crouched, inspecting a blue-black beetle he'd captured in his lunch box. His brow furrowed in a way that Cassandra found funny – it reminded her of the tiny hourglass that popped up when the computer needed time to think.

'Me and Fox aren't really that different.'

'You aren't?'

'No. I think we're the same. We just do things differently. I turn everything outward. He turns everything inward.'

'Hmm.'

Billy frowned. 'You know, sometimes I think you really are from another planet.'

Cassandra still doesn't understand what Billy had meant.

She guesses that this is another way in which he is like a computer – you can see the little hourglass spinning but the calculations going on underneath are hidden.

As she reaches the foot of the stairs which lead up to the roof, Cassandra sees that Billy has already galloped into the night air. When she catches up, she sees the clouds have dissipated and that there is a clear view into the purple, star-pricked heaven beyond.

'Look at all the constellations,' she says, 'not often you see that.'

'It won't last,' he replies.

They go and find the white plastic table where Alice is waiting.

'Thanks for holding some seats for us,' says Billy.

'No biggy,' replies Alice, chugging down a red mouthful from a cocktail jug. 'No one asked for them actually. Tell me, Fran, do I look scary?'

'Yes. Pissed myself the minute I laid eyes on you.'

'Oh fuck you. I'm being serious here. I think those girls over on that table are frightened of me or something. Been giving me horrible looks. What do you think, Cass? Do I look scary?'

Alice is wearing leopard print leggings and a yellowish fake fur coat over a tie-dye tank top. Four gold alphabet rings on her left hand spell out C U N T. While she waits for an answer her fingers absently rip and tear at the label on an empty beer bottle. Cassandra does not know Alice particularly well but has interacted with her enough to realise that under the flamboyant clothes and aggressive banter there is a woman who is deeply insecure. She tries to think of something reassuring to say.

'There is a possibility that someone with poor eyesight might mistake you for a large cat. Other than that you appear only moderately threatening.'

'I don't know why I was expecting a normal answer. How are you all then? Find a job yet, Fran?'

Billy bites his lip and shakes his head.

All of Cassandra's friends work, yet do not have jobs. Fox has an apprenticeship and volunteers at a charity shop. Billy, an internship. Alice does zero-hours contract work with a catering agency. Although all of these things involve many hours of labour and sometimes even pay, none of them are considered 'real' jobs.

Cassandra, conversely, does not work. She is not allowed to. At first, no one would give her a job because she was strange. Then it was decided that she was unfit for work because a doctor said she was mentally unwell. Then the government changed and it was decided that she was actually fit for work and was put on a compulsory placement. But then, when she pitched up for work, her boss told her to go home because she was, in his words, 'a total nutter'. He was however nice enough to not report this to the job centre, so she at least didn't get sanctioned.

A sanction is a thing they do to punish people for not finding a job. It is also a thing they do to foreign dictators who murder people. Cassandra isn't certain if either kind of sanction is effective but she gathers that effectiveness isn't really the point. Like so many of Earth's systems, the purpose of the sanction is to make people feel good. Well, the people who aren't the ones getting sanctioned at least.

Cassandra thinks mankind's entire relationship to labour is very odd and irrational. It has the quality of a surreal performance put on for the enjoyment of no one in particular. Humans work tirelessly, fruitlessly, to keep up an appearance of busyness – as if the hand of some god will sweep them off the planet like verminous insects from a kitchen counter should they idle for too long. She wonders what they will do if all the jobs run out, if all the human work to be done is done. Will they accept this new-found peace or continue performing for their unseen taskmaster, eyes looking fearfully over their shoulders?

A low howl sounds in the distance, deep in the woods of Goregree.

'Old Grey...' The words fall from Billy's lips absently – as if he is talking in his sleep.

Old Grey is a Goregree legend – a roach of immense size

and age who dwells deep in the forest's heart. Billy has always had a strange attraction to the forest bugs and the stories that surround them. His dad was killed by The Cough, a disease that afflicts humans who live too close to the woods or who take too much GOTE. It is caused by poisonous chemicals the insects produce in their wings – wings which are delicate and release tiny translucent fragments into the air whenever they flap. People who come into contact with the bugs inhale these fragments. Over time the poison builds up in their guts, making them cough, vomit, break out in black oozing sores, then die.

Cassandra feels anxious as she watches Billy stare out into the woods.

Then Fox emerges from up the stairs, drinks in hand, and dispels the pensive mood.

'Right,' he says, smiling, laying glasses out on the table. 'Corona for Cass and a Black Death for Billy.'

'A what for me?'

'A Black Death.' Fox pushes the pint towards him. 'It's good.'

'I'll be the judge of that.' Billy sips and immediately gasps. 'It's accurately named, I'll give it that much.'

'What's it like?'

'What do you mean "what's it like?" You said it was good a moment ago – haven't you tasted it before?'

'My review was provisional.'

'Your face is provisional. It tastes like coffee and cold medicine. Drinkable though.'

Cassandra inspects her drink. It is in a long thin glass and has a pink curly straw sticking out of the top. She slowly slides back the visor on her helmet. The cold air against her cheek sends a shiver up her neck. Sticking the straw between her lips, she sucks up a mouthful of Mexican lager.

'Ooooooh my,' says Alice, in a *Carry On* way. 'Now take the rest of it off.'

Billy smiles, gives her a little punch on the shoulder. 'Alice!'

'What? I'm just joking around, Fran.'

'You're creeping. Practically salivating.'

Alice laughs. 'Oh like you're such a bleeding saint. Bloody blokes. All you think about is sex and—'

'Children. Children now,' interrupts Fox. 'I think if you look deep in your hearts you will see that you are *both* creeping creeps who only think about sex.'

'Actually, I think Billy spends most of his time thinking about bugs,' says Cassandra, matter-of-factly.

Everyone gives her a bemused look.

'Oh. My. God,' says Alice, slurping her red drink. 'She's just precious.'

'An angel,' concurs Fox, sipping his green drink.

Cassandra frowns. She has the distinct impression these humans are patronising her.

'Anyway, deep down I'm really all about horse-faced women,' Alice continues, lighting a cigarette. 'Give me a posh woman with a long nose and rabbit teeth and a big house in the country who's got a name like Cherise or some shit.'

'I thought you were all about goblin-faced girls from the council estate called Saphira?' says Fox. 'Also, I'll never fucking understand why you describe people you find attractive in such awful, unflattering terms.'

'I don't expect you to keep up with my complex desires. As far as I can tell you're only attracted to obscure musical artists from the 70s and 80s.'

'I'd hardly call Brian Eno or Patti Smith obscure.'

'Fuck you, you fucking hipster cockasaurus-rex. If it's not on the jukebox in Jawbones it's obscure.'

'But that would include pretty much every—'

'No, no, no, no. Stop talking immediately, you bell-end. You are not allowed to make me feel like any more of a philistine than I already do. I have a hard enough time as it is keeping up with Billy when he burbles on about the noodley abstract crap he listens to. Where's Louie? He's pretty much the only one other than me in our group that listens to normal music. I need moral support.'

'Oh yes,' says Cassandra, 'that reminds me. Louie won't be coming down tonight, he's got a placement.'

The mood around the table deflates. Everyone is quiet for a moment, then Billy's eyes widen. 'Aw bugger,' he says, burying his face in his hands.

'What's wrong?' Cassandra asks.

He gestures to two human males.

Cassandra recognises them from their old school. One is tall, muscular, and wears a sleeveless shirt and baseball cap – its long brim like the voluminous crests that tropical birds use to attract mates. His name is Rhys. The other person is shorter and slimmer. He has skinny jeans and a neatly trimmed beard. His name is Charles.

Billy hates these men.

This is because of a series of incidents that happened during the final year of school.

Increasingly vicious rumours had been circulating in class about Billy's deceased father – a foreigner who everyone knew very little about and who, some suspected, might have been Black, Asian, or Eastern European. At first they started spreading it about that he had been an illegal immigrant. Then they began claiming he was a terrorist. The rumours escalated into pranks, name-calling, more serious name-calling, small acts of violence. Some boys wrote a fake bomb threat and signed it with Billy's name, causing him to be put into counselling. Some others spray-painted 'Paki Fucker' on his mum's car. Then, finally, there was an 'incident' involving Billy, Fox, Charles and Rhys that was so disastrous the school moved in to keep the whole thing quiet and prevent a scandal. After that the situation de-escalated, the rumours went quiet, and normality resumed.

Billy gulps his drink and glares at the men who chat obliviously to each other – drinking and leaning against the wall that circles the perimeter of the roof.

'Say,' says Fox, standing up, having noticed the men as well.

'How about we go downstairs? Maybe dance or something?'

Billy doesn't respond. He takes another big gulp of his drink.

Fox squeezes Billy's shoulder. 'Hey now,' he says. 'It's okay. Come on. Let's go.'

Billy gently pushes Fox's hand away. 'Yeah. Yeah. Sorry, I'm alright.'

As they stand up and leave the table, Cassandra knows that Billy is not alright.

She checks the time on her mobile: 21:30.

Three more hours...

The Lunar Window is another truth that was revealed to her by the film *They Came From Alpha Centauri*. It is a period of the month when the likelihood of abduction is highest. Cassandra had identified it by studying the film and noting down all the times when the characters were rescued. After taking into account the time zones of the film's various settings and making some adjustments, she'd been able to conclude that the hours between midnight and four am were most favourable – these were the hours when four of the film's five characters were safely abducted. The exception to this was the fifth character, Leon, who was the first to be beamed up during the film's climax. Throughout the events of the movie, even though he had forgotten his past alien life on Alpha Centauri, Leon continued to wear his spacesuit at all times. Cassandra interpreted his character as a message that she too must always wear a spacesuit, as a symbol of her faith.

She will be rescued.

She will see her parents again.

It is certain.

SOCIAL

BUTTERFLY\

COMPASS

EYEBROW

The past. School. The secluded spot where Cassandra and Billy, aged fifteen, eat lunch, have stilted conversations, and stare into the grimy pool of rain water.

Fox is not there. He tends to flutter away like this every now and then. Cassandra once overheard someone in class call him a 'social butterfly'. At the time she thought that if Fox were a butterfly he must be a very sad one to be flapping so desperately from place to place, never being still.

There is a crack of twig.

Cassandra turns to see Charles and Rhys approaching, grinning. Rhys is holding something black and shimmering. A bin bag? Charles is absently twirling a roll of duct tape around his finger.

'What do you want?' says Billy.

'Just to ask a few questions,' states Charles.

Rhys suddenly gallops up to Billy and pins him to the ground. 'I've got him,' he says.

'What the hell are you doing? Get off me!' Billy yells.

'Are you resisting arrest?' asks Charles, spinning silver tape around Billy's hands and legs.

'What are you doing?' gasps Cassandra.

'Interrogating a terrorist, madam,' says Charles, smirking. 'Now tell me, Billy – if that is your real name – who was your daddy, where did he come from, what was his mission?'

'Fuck you, Charles.'

Charles stands on Billy's neck and slowly begins to exert pressure, grinding in the heel of his leather school shoe.

Billy squirms. 'I don't know, you bell-end. I've never known. He died when I was five, okay.'

'Tell me, when your dad was fucking your mother, do you think she liked it? Do you think she liked his big black dick in her pussy?'

'I think *your* mum liked it a bit more.'

Charles stamps on his head.

Cassandra snaps out of her daze and bolts across the fields to the cafeteria, nearly tripping over her feet. Weaving through the crowd, she finds Fox talking with some girls, laughing, smiling, gesturing theatrically with his hands. When he sees her his easy smile cracks.

'Cass, what's wrong?'

'It's Billy. Charles and … the rugby boy. I can't remember his name.'

'It doesn't matter. What's going on?'

'They've put duct tape around his arms. They were kicking him. They said they were going to strip him naked.'

Fox's expression hardens in a way that Cassandra has never seen before.

'Alright, I'm going to go kill them,' he says dryly.

'What?'

Fox has already slung his bag over his shoulder and is marching out of the cafeteria.

The other girls at the table are whispering to each other:

'What was that about?'

'Something about Charles and that creep Billy?'

'I heard his dad was a Muslim.'

'In al-Qaeda?'

'Yeah, like a proper one from Iraq and everything.'

'Nah, I heard he was some sort of Polish gyppo. Knocked up a British girl and then stayed here living off benefits.'

Cassandra tunes out their gossip and tries to focus. She feels so disorientated. When she thinks about that boy stamping on Billy's head her brain freezes up – as if she can't process it. Spotting a teacher by the entrance, she runs to him, grabs him by the arm.

'Mr Mathews,' she blurts, 'I need your help, it's urgent!'

'Is it ever not? What's the trouble, Cassandra?'

'Charles and this other boy from our class – Rhys! That was his name! – are beating up Billy and calling him a terrorist and pinning him to the ground and tying him up. I told Fox and now he's going to go stop them but I'm worried he might go too far.'

'Fox? Oh no,' he mutters. 'Okay, take me there immediately.'

Cassandra leads Mr Mathews across the fields, through the trees, to where she and Billy had only ten minutes before been eating their lunch in peaceful silence.

Everything seems to be moving slowly, as if she is a tiny insect for whom a day is a lifetime.

Billy is lying on the moist muddy ground, a bin bag over his head, his trousers and pants pulled down to reveal a flaccid penis and skinny thighs. From head to toe he is splashed in a clear liquid she knows, from the smell, to be urine.

Rhys is standing still, a compass lodged through his eyebrow, looking in dumb incomprehension at the blood that is pouring out of him.

Charles is on his back, crying, covered in bruises that are slowly rising out of his face like dough cooking in an oven.

On top of him, fists raised, Fox's expression is glacial.

Before he can bring down his fist again, the teacher begins shouting, 'If you don't get off him right this instant I will bounce you into juvenile detention so fast it will break the sound barrier!'

Fox sighs, stands up, and walks over to Billy.

'Could you pass me back my compass, Rhys?' he says.

Rhys, bewildered, nods and hands it over.

Fox begins using the compass needle to rip the duct tape off of Billy's arms and legs.

The teacher exhales sharply. Hands shaking, he pulls a cigarette out from his pocket. He barely gets through a tenth of it before dropping and squashing it into the grass.

'Okay. Listen up you three. For now, this didn't happen. I'm taking these two to the nurse and as far as explanations go, you kids were climbing trees and fell over.'

'What about Billy?' asked Cassandra.

'What about him?'

'He's really beat up. We should take him to the nurse's office too.'

'No. I don't want that boy, or that little chav psycho next to him, to even be on the same premises as Charles at the moment. If his injuries are bad then take him to a hospital. And remember – he fell out of a tree.'

'But they started it!'

'Frankly, I don't care who started what. Do what I say if you don't want to end up in trouble.'

And with that, the teacher leads the bullies away along a circuitous route, away from the clusters of children who are slowly drifting back towards the classrooms.

As he disappears into the central school building, Cassandra realises she has no idea where the nearest hospital is or how to get there. She wonders for a moment where she can find a phonebook, or maybe a map of the local area.

Her thoughts are interrupted by the sound of Fox crying.

She turns to see that he has got the bag off and now has his arms wrapped around Billy whose grouchy expression is about the same as usual.

'Bell-end,' Billy murmurs. 'You know I'm covered in piss, right?'

HOMEFREE\
PAINFUL
HISTORIES

It is around eleven when Cassandra notices a red stain on the back of her spacesuit.

'My bum is bleeding,' she says to no one in particular. Her friends have all recently dispersed. Fox is dancing, Billy is at the bar, and Alice has disappeared to places unknown.

Cassandra prods the wet patch. It is warm.

Deciding this is something that needs further attention, she walks through the throbbing haze of humans to the ladies'. It is surprisingly empty and quiet – the insulation muffles the club's throbbing bass music. The room consists of six cubicles and a large mirror with three sinks below it. One of the sinks contains a vomit-filled vodka bottle that briefly attracts Cassandra's awe. How did they manage to fill it so completely with such limited spillage?

Trying the first cubicle, she opens then quickly closes the door, briefly glimpsing what appears to be a football-sized roach laying dead in the toilet bowl. The second cubicle is clean. Or at least relatively clean. There are some loose sheets of toilet roll on the floor and a tiny splash of urine in the corner, but it is usable. She gets in, unzips her spacesuit and inspects her behind. Just below the left cheek, extending down her thin pale leg, she can see a large, swollen blob of reddish purple. Poking it with her finger she realises the whole area is worryingly numb. It seems the taxi did damage to her after all. Cassandra feels irritated. In a way it doesn't matter – when she is beamed to Alpha Centauri she will leave this body behind. But still, she wants to be clean and undamaged when the spaceship comes.

Using some loo paper, Cassandra mops up what she

can of the blood. It has mostly coagulated into a sticky goo. Satisfied, she has a quick piss, zips up and steps out of the toilet just in time to see Alice puke red ooze into a sink.

'Yuck,' Alice squawks, splattering droplets of vomit on the mirror. 'Fuck me that's vile. Looks like it's wriggling.'

Alice has taken off her fur coat and Cassandra can't help but stare at the swollen black sore on her exposed shoulder.

'Oh, hey, Cass. What you gawking at? Oh. This. Look, just don't tell Billy. He'd freak. He's a bit of a delicate boy really.' Alice lets out a harsh rasping cough that sounds like someone sawing wood with a rusty blade. As she hacks and splutters, the veins under the black poison mark throb like a second swollen heart.

Cassandra grimaces.

'Hey, don't look too disgusted. It's not nice to make a woman feel ugly.'

'Sorry. I didn't mean to. I don't think you're ugly at all.'

'Ha. Then why are you so cold?' Alice takes a cigarette out of her fur coat. Her fingers tremble. 'Fuck,' she says, lighting up.

Cassandra turns her head to the side, pulling her eyes away from the smoke.

'So tell me,' continues Alice. 'What's your angle?'

'Huh?'

'You playing hard to get? Going for that androgynous-mystery-girl-sort-of-vibe? I mean, I've known you for nearly a year now and I've never quite figured out how much of the spacesuit thing is an act.'

Cassandra raises an eyebrow. She shuffles back an inch, her space boots making an audible squeak on the gungy floor.

'Hey,' says Alice, a bit of spit and vomit dribbling from the corner of her mouth. 'Don't take it like that. I don't mean it aggressively. I just want to be let in a bit. Who are you interested in? Is it one of the boys? Please don't tell me it's Billy. He's lovely but he's got issues.'

'Interested in?'

'Argh. Stop playing at being dense. Who do you want to fuck? Look, I won't tell a soul. Just talk to me. In all the time I've known you, you've barely said a word to me.'

'I don't really want to have sex with anyone, Alice.'

'Oh come on. I don't buy that at all. I mean, I don't blame you if no one around here floats your boat but surely—'

'You don't understand,' snaps Cassandra. 'Nothing floats my boat. My boat has never once floated for the entire time that I've been...'

'Maybe,' says Alice, leaning in, reaching for Cassandra's hand. 'But maybe. Perhaps.'

Alice moves in to kiss.

Cassandra pulls away.

Alice frowns and looks at the floor. Then she laughs.

'Fuck,' she says, sucking on her cigarette. 'I always crush on the straight ones. Sorry. I'm a drunken mess.'

'It's okay, Alice. I understand.'

'What I don't get is ... well why do you even come out? I mean, nothing floats your boat. All you care about is going back to space. Yet here you are in this club. drinking. And you follow Billy and Fox around as if they might die if you take your eyes off them for even a moment.'

'Shut up!' Cassandra is as surprised as Alice to hear those words roaring out of her mouth at a volume she didn't know she could speak. 'Sorry,' she says. 'I don't know where that came from.'

'No worries,' says Alice. 'I hit a nerve there. I should stop running my mouth. And actually it all makes sense really. I guess it doesn't matter whether you're from Earth or space, we all cope with shit in the same stupid ways...' Alice trails off, looking upward as if searching for an answer to a question. Then she giggles. 'You know, it's like this whole fucking town has abandonment issues... Ugh sorry, Cass. I'm out of it. Could I scooch past and use the sink behind you? Mine's full of sick.'

'Certainly,' says Cassandra, moving towards the door. 'Anyway, I'm going to step out now.' She exhales sharply as she leaves, her visor still cloudy from Alice's breath.

All around, bleary-eyed humans sway in the stale club air to music that is noisy but not in a way that is audacious or interesting. Rather it is mundane, punishing – like the sound of pavement being torn up by industrial machines or the din of traffic. It is in moments like this that Cassandra really hates the human obsession with bad chemicals and the bad ideas those chemicals nurture.

She finds Billy with Fox standing by an air conditioner near the bar.

'Hey, Cass,' says Billy, 'was wondering where you were. Bugger me, this place stinks of sweat. Never thought I'd miss the days before the smoking ban. Anyway, we should get a move on.'

'We're going to see the farmer!' lilts Fox woozily.

'Excuse me?' asks Cassandra.

'F. A. R. M. R. Farmer!'

'You missed the "e".'

'I did no such thing.'

'Billy, what is he talking about?'

'Fox and me are going to get some GOTE. Know it's not exactly your scene but it'd be nice if you could join us.'

Cassandra opens her mouth to say no. To say that she is feeling tired and it is probably time she called it an evening. Time to wave goodbye to Earth.

Instead, for reasons she doesn't understand, the words, 'Yes. I think I can tag along for a short while' come out and once they are out she doesn't have the heart to tuck them back in.

'Cool,' says Fox. 'Are we waiting for Alice?'

'Nah,' replies Billy, wincing, gripping the bridge of his nose as if he has a headache. 'Nah. She texted to say she was heading home – not feeling well.'

Cassandra wonders if Alice had sent that message before or after their uncomfortable encounter in the toilets.

'Alright, comrades,' slurs Fox, dribbling a bit of drink down his chin. 'Let's be on our merry way then.'

When they reach the entrance, the bald bouncer standing watch by the door sheepishly says, 'Sorry about before, Miss.'

Looking up, Cassandra realises he is the man from earlier. The new guy. Seeing him now, she gets a different impression of him. His expression is softer, his cheeks babyish – like some hairless, playdough human made by a child. She nods and shuffles into the lift.

Fox giggles. 'I think that bouncer was into you.'

'Come on, Fox,' scolds Billy. 'Don't be a dick now.'

'I mean he wanted you, Cass. Could see it in his eyes. Couldn't you tell? Bloke was thirsty.'

Cassandra looks down at her orange space boots. 'I really, really wish humans would stop asking things from me that I can't give.'

For a minute or so the only sounds in the lift are the whir of machinery and the creak of the glass cube lift swaying in the wind ever so slightly.

'Sorry, Cass,' says Fox. 'That was a stupid thing to say. I know you're not comfortable talking about that sort of—'

'Then please don't.'

Fox nods.

The lift lands with a grinding squeal and the Orphan Three step out into the blustery night, proceeding in silence down the road – Fox in front, Billy just after, and Cassandra at the rear, close behind yet a little apart.

After a few minutes, Billy gestures to a small corner shop. 'Just going to pop in here.'

'Sure,' says Fox, sitting down on a nearby bench, stretching out his arms. 'I'll wait outside.'

Billy steps inside. Cassandra scrapes her boots on the welcome mat and follows in after.

The interior consists of two disorganised aisles and a counter with a single till, above which hovers the decaying symbol of some ubiquitous corporate chain – a white smiley on a blue background circled by the text HOMEFREE. A

81

woman with a scraped back ponytail in an ill-fitting green uniform slouches behind the till, tapping her fingers absently on the counter. For a moment her eyes shut and it looks like she might fall asleep right there and then. Then she startles awake as if from a bad dream. She resumes tapping on the counter and swallows a yawn. As she does so, the smiling logo above her takes on a different aspect to Cassandra. Its grin no longer seems friendly but malicious, as if laughing at its human servant below.

Clank.

There is a rustle of bottles as, across the shop, Billy fumbles trying to pick a bottle from the top shelf.

'Need any help, love?' the shopkeeper asks.

'No, no. I'm fine. Thank you,' replies Billy, straightening up the display.

Cassandra wanders over to the confectionery section and selects a few things. Then she goes to the counter and plonks down a green bottle of pop and a bag of mixed sweets. The sweets are yellow and blue and shaped like spacemen. They are the sort Cassandra's foster carer used to buy her when she'd been well-behaved – her definition of well-behaved being 'quiet and not talking about Alpha Centauri.'

The woman behind the till scans her items. 'Isn't it hot in that thing?' she asks.

'Relatively breezy actually.'

'Ah. Yes,' she says, stuffing Cassandra's purchase in a bag and handing it over.

She thanks the woman, steps away and allows Billy room to place his items on the counter – a bottle of ale and a milky bar.

'Could you get me a pack of Richmond, and a lighter as well please?'

The shopkeeper scans the items and shoves them into a bag. Then, as she is handing them over, her eyes widen with recognition. 'Hey!' she gasps. 'You're Liz's son aren't you?'

Billy winces at the mention of his mother's name. Cassandra has only met the woman once. She is an emotionally withdrawn human. Not cold, but definitely distant – always drifting away from the world, staring into nothing, which is perfectly understandable really.

'I went to school with Liz,' continues the woman. 'Oh it was terrible what happened to your dad. Of course, he was one of the first, now wasn't he? To get The Cough.'

'Please. It's... It's not something I like to...'

'Oh. I'm sorry,' she says. 'Say no more. I won't carry on. I just want to say...' She trails off, bites her lip. 'It was really truly awful what happened to your father. But, you know, God sends these things to try us, love. I think these sorts of things happen for a reason.'

Billy's thick eyebrows draw tight like a bowstring. 'Oh get stuffed!' he says. 'These sorts of things happen for a reason? What a crock. If you want to think that, if that's what gets you to sleep at night, then fine – but keep that feel-good, bright-side crap to yourself. Because I know from personal fucking experience that there is not one single scrap of meaning in any of the shit that Dad went through, that Mum went through, that I went through. It was all pointless. One day my dad was there. And then he was... Sorry.'

'No worries, love,' says the shopkeeper, giving him a wary look.

Billy quickly marches out through the door, his plastic bag of chocolate and ale swinging by his side, perilously close to the ground.

'That boy needs some serious help.'

Cassandra isn't certain if the shopkeeper is talking to her, to herself, or to some unseen entity. Above them, the white HOMEFREE smiley really does seem to be laughing.

She waves to the shopkeeper and steps outside to see Billy sitting cross-legged on the pavement – his eyes closed, his nostrils wheezing as heavy breaths go through them.

Fox nudges her in the stomach. 'What happened in there?' he asks.

'He lost his temper with the woman behind the till.'

'What? Why?'

'She said some stuff about his father.'

'Oh no. Well. Let's give him a moment.'

'It's okay,' says Billy, standing up. 'I just needed to clear my head. No need to worry.'

'You sure, mate? We can call it an evening if you're not feeling so good.'

'No. No it's all fine. Let's press on. Lead the way, man.'

And so they set off down the street in their habitual Orphan Three formation – Fox in the front, Billy in the middle, Cassandra at the back.

As they walk in silence down the cold, crisp Goregree streets, Cassandra wonders why she hasn't gone home yet. Why has she said yes and agreed to stay out longer with the boys when the Lunar Window is so close to opening? Why risk it?

She also thinks about what Alice had said: abandonment issues. She had overheard her foster carer talking about that once to a woman from Social Services. About how being abandoned by a primary carer at a young age can make some humans cling irrationally to other humans, in case they too might disappear in an instant. Can make some humans avoid new experiences, avoid change. Cassandra has always wondered who her foster carer was referring to back then. It couldn't have been her. She was never abandoned after all. Her parents are coming to get her.

'So what did you guys get?' asks Fox, breaking the silence.

'Sweets,' says Cassandra.

'Booze. Smokes,' says Billy, lighting up one of his cigarettes.

Fox grins. 'I thought you'd quit?' he says.

'I did. This is what you call a relapse.'

'Is that so?'

'Fox, I want to get so fucking high tonight.'

'That's the spirit. Come on, we've got to make a left here.'

As they turn the corner and enter a new part of town, the house and shop and street lights become sparser and sparser until all Cassandra can see are black silhouettes rippling atop an ocean of purple night. They are approaching the old town centre that was left derelict many, many years ago. Cassandra isn't certain why it was left to crumble. Some say it was because it was too close to the woods, to the roaches, to the source of The Cough. But others say it was abandoned much sooner than that. That it was left because it spoke to a painful history. The concrete blocks of Goregree are full of such histories, many of which contradict each other.

One such story says that when Dean Fritz's builders came to lay the foundations for Goregree they found an abandoned town not on any maps – an omen, perhaps, of what was to come. Another story said that, rather than being a doomed but well-intentioned enterprise, the building of Goregree had been destructive from the start, that villages and communities which had existed for centuries were sucked unwillingly into the project.

Another even older tale says that, long before any settlements had been built, the area that would become Goregree had been the location of a remote mental institution where horrible experiments had taken place. 'A prison full of nutters' as Cassandra heard one person describe it. A person who went on to joke that not much had really changed since.

Cassandra doesn't know if any of these stories are true, but the air is thick with them; a disorienting fog.

JUNK HEAD
ALICE\SNAKE
VOICE SIMON

After the embarrassing incident with Cassandra in the bathroom, Alice knows it is probably best to go home. I mean, after a fuck up like that you ought to call it quits, holster your guns, and live to fight another day. Instead, as she exits the elevator of the Enterprise, Alice starts jabbing the number of her dealer friend into her smart phone. Smart phones: allowing dumb people to make dumb decisions all damn dumb day long.

She puts the receiver to her ear and drawls, 'Hey, Simon, fancy meeting up for a quick one? I'll bring the beers if you bring the GOTE...' and before she knows it she is in the passenger seat of Simon's crap-heap of a car – derivatively engraved along the side with the name 'Pussy Wagon' – a four pack of cheap off-brand lager squeezed between her now shivering thighs. Shivering from cold, or booze, or regret? Alice does not know. Simon looks about the same as he always does. Metallica t-shirt, jeans, goatee, blond hair tied back in a ponytail. Biceps like a man who likes to lift. Gut like a man who likes chips. She calls him her dealer friend but it is more accurate to say that he is her parents' dealer friend. He is about twice her age and she's known him since she was ten.

'Heard anything from your parents?' His voice is surprisingly high pitched for a man of his size.

'Nah,' she replies.

That is the end of their conversation.

Alice and Simon get on like a house on fire – that is, like a building where everyone inside is trying to escape while being suffocated by searing black smoke. Alice isn't certain what the black smoke represents in this metaphor. Their awkward lack of anything in common other than drink and drugs? The conceit probably needs more work.

Alice and Simon have only two things that truly connect them – bad chemicals and a shared history of awkward encounters.

The first such encounter was at a family barbecue when Alice's mother, incredibly high and talking to her twelve-year-old daughter as if she were six, introduced Simon to her as 'Uncle Simon' and continued to refer to him as 'Uncle Simon' for the rest of the day. She then announced that actually 'Uncle Simon' was an old boyfriend and could've ended up being 'Daddy Simon' if she hadn't met her husband. Alice's mother thought this was a hilarious observation. Alice's father also thought so because he thought every observation Alice's mum made was hilarious, and she thought the same of him, and they were both insufferable together. Alice found the whole situation excruciating. And yet that was not actually the most toe-curling encounter she'd had with the man. That award went to a moment in Enterprise six years later when he, not realising who she was, offered to finger her – creatively suggesting that, in return, she could suck his dick. When she revealed who she was he launched into a deluge of apologies. Explained that it had been a few years since he had last seen her and didn't recognise her. That in the dark, she looked like a woman he had been talking to before he left to take a piss. That he would never proposition an old friend's daughter. Not that she didn't look very attractive. Not that he was into teens, mind you. And so on and on and on Simon went for twenty painful minutes, during which, the mental image of herself clambering over his pot belly in search of his penis while he jabbed his hairy fingers into her, took up permanent residence in Alice's mind.

Given this history of cringe encounters, Alice finds it strange that Simon even wants to be in the same postcode as her. Her reason for continuing their awkward acquaintance is obvious. She wants GOTE. Simon sells GOTE. Cheaply, quickly, and conveniently as well. But his reasoning is more opaque. Why put himself through so much discomfort? Perhaps it is out of some lingering loyalty to her parents? Or maybe he is one of those guys who just doesn't know how to say no to a woman he finds attractive? She certainly got that vibe seeing his interactions with her mum. Perhaps he is lonely. Or perhaps she is projecting. Maybe he just sees her as a long-time customer he has some colourful history with. Or maybe he thinks if he gets her drunk or high enough then she will suck his dick. Maybe this is all part of a conspiracy Simon set in motion to get his dick sucked. Maybe she is being paranoid and overthinking things. Yes. That last one, Alice thinks. That seems to be on the money.

Burping quietly into her hand, she attempts to open one of the lager cans. Clasping her thumb and finger around the tab, she levers it upward.

Pop.

The tab rips off. The lager can remains unopened.

Bugger.

Rummaging in the cubbyhole, she finds a pen knife with what appears to be a spunking dick doodled in Tipp-Ex on the side. Repressing a giggle, she unfurls one of the knife's many appendages. A corkscrew? That will do. She punches in the scored part of the lid. Is there a name for that? Before the question is even fully formed in her brain, Alice has her phone out and is doing an internet search. Fifteen minutes later she knows a rough history of aluminium beverage can design.

Alice's brain is full of junk. She guesses that makes sense – being a junkie and all.

'Say,' says Simon, his soft breathy voice emphasising and stretching out the 'ay' in a way which reminds her of something, but she isn't sure what. 'How about we go some place different for a change? I was just thinking. Seeing as it's a little closer. We could go to the farm. It's real serene at this time of night, like. There's this very zen field full of dandelions. And I can show you how we make the GOTE.'

Alice shrugs. 'Yeah. Sure.'

The snake from *The Jungle Book*. That is what Simon's voice reminds her of. The black sore on her neck begins to itch.

Sweat? Semen?\ Virgin Rice Cracker

'So...' says Jen, 'actually fancy some of that GOTE now?'

Louie shakes his head.

'Suit yourself. Now where did I put my pipe?'

She turns her naked back on Louie and rummages in a bedside drawer. Minutes before, that back had filled him with fire but now it is just a back. Pallid. Thin skin with blue veins showing through. A 5p-sized bump of red acne just below the neck. The back of a short woman in her early thirties illuminated by a slightly-dimmed light.

'Hmm. I think I left it in the car. Oh well. Want a drink?'

'Yeah. I guess. Thanks.'

Jen gets out of the bed, slips into some slippers, and walks to the adjacent kitchen. There is no wall between the two rooms. In fact all the rooms in Jen's flat, except the bathroom, are combined into one big space that feels stitched together and awkward. Beige carpeting that abruptly gives way to chequered tiles. Mismatched wallpaper. Exposed masonry. It is as if some previous owner had once had aspirations of joining all these rooms together cohesively but had only got as far as knocking down the walls before giving up.

As Jen steps into the slightly brighter kitchen, there is a shimmer along her thigh as the light catches some fluid clinging to her leg hairs. Cum or sweat? wonders Louie. Cum and sweat? It is hard to say. Everything has happened very quickly. And now the air smells of his cum, their sweat, and her mint-flavoured e-cigarette.

'Carlsberg okay?'

'Yup.'

'Good. Because it's all I got.'

Jen brings over two cans and sits down next to him on the bed.

'So, Louie,' she says, cracking open her can and handing the other to him. 'Are you a virgin?'

Louie gives her a confused look.

'I mean were you a virgin? Before tonight?'

Louie nods.

'Thought as much.'

'Why?' Louie says, fiddling roughly with the tab on his can before finally pulling it open. 'Was I crap or something?'

'Not really. You just sort of gave off that vibe. You were alright... Sorry, that was damning with faint praise. I'm not the best person to talk to about these things. My relationship with sex is a bit odd.'

'How so?'

'Well...' Jen sucks up a mouthful of lager and seems to consider her words. 'I suppose it's a bit like how some people are with junk food. No actually not so much junk food as bland food – like rice crackers or something. It's not exactly nutritional, you're not even sure if you enjoy the taste, but when the opportunity to have one pops up ... well you don't even think about it, you just sort of compulsively eat them.' She pauses to have another swig of her lager. 'Hmm. Though come to think of it maybe it's not quite like rice crackers at all. Rice crackers are consistently bland but sex is sometimes pretty great. Also sometimes pretty awful. Maybe sex for me is more like scratch cards. Most of the time you don't get much out of it – just cardboard and disappointment. But you keep rolling the dice for that occasional time when you feel like it's more than just two meat dolls rolling around on a mattress. Are you following me?'

'Yes,' says Louie slowly. 'So what you're saying is that I'm a virgin rice cracker you took a gamble on?'

'I think you're making fun of me and I don't like it.' Jen goes quiet for a moment, appears to ruminate on something. She strokes her hand along Louie's thigh, a sensation he finds tickles. At a glance Jen looks girlish but her hands tell a different story. They are coarse, slightly wrinkled, veiny, a little cool. They remind Louie of another hand.

Suddenly, appearing to reach some kind of conclusion in her head, Jen stands up. 'Anyway, this was nice but we should probably not make this a thing, Louie. I mean you're like what – seventeen or something?'

'Nineteen.'

'Oh. Either way I'm still probably old enough to be your mum. And at any rate it wouldn't look good to my company – me sleeping with some kid sent to us on a placement. You'll keep this to yourself, will you?'

'Yes,' he replies.

'You will? I'll be in shit if you started gobbing off about this.'

'I promise I won't tell,' he says. 'I...' Internally he finishes the sentence— '...will be dead tomorrow anyway.'

'Lovely.' Jen smiles, finishing the last of her lager and crushing the can. 'No hard feelings I hope? I'll call you a cab.'

Jen picks up her mobile from the bedside table and turns away from him.

From behind, at this angle, all Louie can see of her are her two ivory-white calves sticking out from beneath a waterfall of damp black hair. She looks in the dim light like one of those ghost women from Japanese folklore that Louie has seen in films – Yuuray? Wuurey? Yurei? What is it again?

Jen slips and drops her scrunched up lager can. Still talking to the taxi driver, she crouches down on the floor to pick it up. As she does this her legs vanish beneath her dark waterfall hair. And all Louie can see, all that is left of her, is that mass of black. She becomes a black hole in the carpet, shrinking downwards, as if she might disappear.

Empty Vessels\

Treacherous Feet

As the Orphan Three progress down the road, buildings give way to vegetation and tarmac fades to dirt-track. They are approaching the castle – the rendezvous point where Fox's mysterious 'farmer' will meet them to exchange money for GOTE. The air is tinted with mist and the trees are densely packed. Every time Cassandra sees these looming oaks she is reminded of the Germanic forests of legend – woods that devoured Roman legions whole.

She checks her mobile. She hopes the boys will consume their GOTE quickly. By her estimation, the Lunar Window has begun to open. In another hour or so the scanner signals from the Alpha Centaurian spaceship, which have the power to transmit alien souls, will reach their peak resonance and clarity.

Eventually, they arrive at the castle, which, despite its name, is little more than a few loose, wall-like arrangements of moss-covered stones blasted by the elements. The ruins are from a hazy period. Speculation on their origins is wild and fanciful. The wizard's tower of the great cambion Merlin? The remnants of an alien outpost? An elaborate hoax? No one knows for certain.

Parked nearby is a rickety pickup truck – the lights of which are the only illumination besides the stars and moon. Standing next to the vehicle is a large muttering man, with muscular ham-sized arms and a bushy red beard that curls upwards like a horn. His white shirt, which barely conceals his bulging chest and gut, has a big red heart on it. Cassandra gathers that this is Fox's farmer.

'Have you brought the stuff?' Fox asks in a hushed, faux

American accent.

'Cute,' replies the farmer, scratching his belly. 'You actually got the cash this time, Fox? If you're short like last time I promise I will get back in my truck and leave.'

'It's okay, man. I got everything this time and a little extra. No need to worry.'

'Nice. I'll get your "stuff" then.' As he says 'stuff' the farmer rolls his eyes and does little rabbits with his fingers for emphasis. Then he leans into the truck and pulls out something wrapped in brown paper. It is about the size of a rugby ball and the underside is dripping with unknown fluids. 'Here's your order.'

'Cool.' Fox hands him two twenty pound notes. 'What do I owe you?'

'Cunt, do I look like I can't count? I specifically said it'd be sixty.'

'Oh. I'm sorry. It's so dark out. I thought I handed you three of those.'

'Yeah. I bet you did.'

He passes the man another twenty.

'Okay. You kids have fun then.' The farmer climbs into his vehicle and cranks the ignition. The engine lets out a raspy purr. 'You know you're lucky I'm a nice guy, Fox. There's no way I'd agree to meet at this hour and this location otherwise. Promise me if another dealer offers to meet you so far out of town you tell them to fuck off because you'll end up getting robbed. Or worse – in pieces. Next time you want to buy some GOTE, don't try to be so fucking clever – meet me at the petrol station like a normal person.'

'I'm glad to know you care, man.'

'A farmer needs to watch after his flock.'

'Now look who's being cute – you nick that line from a movie?'

The farmer hits the accelerator and drives off, the glow of his pickup disappearing into the night. The Orphan Three are left only with starlight and the faint yellow glimmer of roach eyes peering out from the trees.

'If I'm following what that man said clearly,' says Billy, lighting up another cigarette, 'then we just spent thirty minutes walking into the middle of bum-fuck nowhere when we could've just gone to the station up by market street.'

'We were going to have to come here anyway,' replies Fox, tossing the package of GOTE back and forth between his left and right hand.

'Why?'

'Because no one comes here and I want to try out Pasting.'

'Fuck me, Fox. You sure? That shit is super dangerous.'

'Hey – you were the one who said you wanted to get super high tonight.'

Billy goes quiet, puffs on his cigarette. In the wavering flicker of that pin-prick flame he is little more than a shape to Cassandra, a shadow with eyes that catch the moonlight, eyes like grey pearls on the deepest floor of the ocean. As each second of silence passes, he seems more distant and ephemeral.

'Yeah. Stuff it,' he says. 'You're right.'

'Aren't I always?' says Fox. 'Anyway, we need a fire or we won't be able to see what the fuck we're doing.'

'We could use our phones?' says Cassandra.

'Cass, you have no sense of romance or atmosphere do you?'

And so the Orphan Three set about collecting wood for a fire which they pile in a circle by one of the castle's ruinous walls. After they have gathered enough tinder, Billy pulls out his lighter, plucks up a thin dry stick, then brings the two together like a child making their dolls kiss.

'Bloody thing,' he grumbles, thumb rubbing ineffectually against the spark wheel. 'Can never get these things to work.'

'It's because you're always pissed whenever you drink,' says Fox, sitting cross-legged in front of the woodpile. 'I mean smoke!' he corrects. 'Ha! Guess I'm pretty hammered myself.' He lets out another of his croaky goose-laughs.

'Yeah,' agrees Billy. 'Way more than I—'. Before he can finish that thought, Billy slips and falls on his back.

Cassandra takes the lighter from his hands and in one simple flick turns it on. She then sets alight the twig and throws it into the pile. After a minute or so they have a healthy flame.

'Lol. Cassandra showing us up again,' says Fox.

'It's easy to show up people when you're sober,' says Billy. 'Also, did you seriously just say lol? Fuck me. Next you'll be saying omg.'

'It's hard to be sober though – especially in this town. And I don't really like verbalising omg as oh em gee. I prefer to say omguh.'

'Huh? Why?'

'Because that's how omg reads phonetically to me – omguh.'

'Okay then,' says Billy, raising his bottle of ale. 'Praise be to great Omguh.' He chugs the last of his drink and wipes his mouth on his wrist. Crumbs of Milky Bar which have been clinging to the corner of his lip smear over his cheek. 'Anyway,' he continues, 'let's do this thing already.'

Fox slowly unfurls the package revealing a blackened, dripping, shrunken animal foetus. Perhaps a baby sheep or calf? It is hard to tell. He gives it an inquisitive prod. Green blood bubbles up from its tiny eyes. This is GOTE, the most prized of all of Goregree's bad chemicals, in its rawest form. It is created when pregnant animals, typically livestock, eat roaches of the forest, poisoning their unborn offspring. This was probably something that happened accidentally at first but, once it was known that the blood of these stillborn animals had hallucinogenic properties, people learned how to repeat the process, mass produce the substance, and package it in different forms. Typically, it is heavily diluted, mixed with thickening agents, and cut with weed or tobacco. This stuff, however, is pure. Smoking it would lead to a quick death. It has to be consumed in a less conventional manner.

'Well. I guess I'll go first seeing as it was my idea,' says Fox, taking off his jacket and shirt to reveal his toned hairless chest.

He dips his fingers into the dead animal's oozing soft body and spreads the GOTE over his thin arms, his gaunt cheeks, his pink nipples, his pale stomach. As green liquid sinks into his skin, his eyes grow wider and wider, as if they want to suck the world into their black irises. Then, Fox reaches round, as if hugging himself, and smooths the stinking blood into his bony shoulders and sides. That done, he shuffles around on his bottom and exposes his back to the others.

'Billy, could you get the rest of me?'

Billy edges closer, scoops up a little of the GOTE, and begins smoothing it into Fox's bare back.

Fox gasps.

Cassandra thinks her friends look like two monkeys grooming each other. She yawns and sits on the ground. There is a wave of exhaustion creeping up through her legs. She wonders again why she's come along. She has no interest in drugs. She could've been on her way to Alpha Centauri right now. But for some reason, whenever she thinks of leaving Billy and Fox, her mind drifts back to that incident at school – the image of that compass lodged in Rhys' eyebrow appearing to her again and again. Is this some primitive herding instinct bubbling up from her human body? Human feelings are mysterious. Mysterious and treacherous.

Slowly, she lays down her head on the dirt and falls into a short fitful dream, or perhaps a memory? Old memories often have an unreal, detached quality to them, like dreams. And dreams are often fractured and incomplete – like memories. Both writhe with bad ideas wishing to be born.

It starts like this:

Cassandra is in her *Ninja Turtle* pyjamas, trying to open the bathroom door. Her mum still hasn't come out. It isn't unusual for her to spend a long time in the bath, especially after Cassandra's dad disappeared, but three hours is a while even for her, and the typical blaring of 'Bohemian Rhapsody', accompanied by her mother's low off-key voice, is nowhere to be heard.

Cassandra knocks. 'Mum, are you okay?' she asks.

No reply.

She knocks again.

And calls again.

And knocks and calls again.

Still no response.

Panic and adrenaline flood Cassandra's synapses.

What if she's fallen asleep and drowned – sucked all the dirty bathwater into her nose and lungs? What if she's slipped and cracked her head, spilling crimson over the bathroom in spiralling little rivers? What if a murderer came in through the window and killed her – slit her throat, ripped out her liver, pierced her kidneys with a long thin stiletto-blade over and over and over and over?

The possibilities are endless, horribly endless.

Cassandra bangs her tiny pink fist against the door until it is red and bruised, then she rattles the handle as hard as she can. Every second the door seems to grow more solid, more imposing, implacable, immovable.

Thump. Thump. Thump.

Cassandra can barely breathe.

She falls to her knees.

Another thought: what if her mother is still alive but just barely holding on, crawling along the floor, desperately trying to reach the door handle as all her organs and limbs and neurones shut down one after one after one?

Cassandra screams, throws her body against the door over and over until her shoulder is aching, stinging, purple with bruises.

Her eyes burn.

She starts to cry.

Then the door creaks open.

Beyond, Cassandra can see her mother's arm hanging limp along the side of the tub with an incredible unearthly stillness, an almost illegible note scribbled in ink along its white flesh –

probably just an item she needed to remember when she was down the shops the other day. Bloody Soy Milk. Yes, it says Bloody Soy Milk and there are three exclamation marks after. Like this—!!!

Cassandra's eyes can't bear to see any more, but her treacherous human feet keep stepping forward. Before long she is hovering over the tub where her mother lies in water dirtied with blood. Her cheeks bloated. Her blue eyes turned upward to the ceiling and the sky and the heavens above.

Cassandra does not scream.

She stops crying.

She stares in silence at her mother's vacant expression. Thinks how much like an empty bottle her corpse is – a vessel shrugged off by its host.

She reaches out to her mother's eyes, believing for a moment that if she shuts them she can stop her soul from leaving.

Then she is awake.

Awake and alone – Billy and Fox nowhere to be seen, the fire faded to embers.

She checks her mobile. She's been asleep for about half an hour.

Where on earth have the boys gone to?

There is a murmur out in the dark.

Standing up, Cassandra switches her phone to torch mode and walks slowly and quietly in the direction of the sound.

Eventually she finds herself back by the road. There is a figure lying there on its side – twitching, convulsing. She turns her phone's blue gaze onto the shape.

'Fox?'

'Oh ... hey, Cass,' he whispers back. 'I'm. I'm not feeling so good.' He is practically naked, with only green GOTE and his boxers covering his pale, shivering body.

'Can you stand?' she asks. 'Here, let me help you up.'

Cassandra lifts him onto his feet.

Fox stumbles, swings his arm around her neck and rests his weight on her.

Cassandra is shocked to find that he is so light – light as a ghost or a thought.

'Where are your clothes?' she asks.

'I don't know,' he says. 'Look. You need to find Billy. He ran off into the woods. I think he might do something.'

'Do what?'

There is a groan in the distance. A low, grinding groan that seems to rumble up through the ground. The cry of Old Grey.

'Okay,' says Cassandra. 'First I'm going to call you a taxi. Then I'm going to go find Billy.' She drags Fox to a tree by the road and lays him down.

'I'm so tired, Cass,' he mumbles. 'So tired.'

She hammers a number into her mobile and puts the receiver to her ear – or at least as close to her ear as the space helmet will allow.

'Hey. Can I get a taxi for my friend from the castle to 93 Princess Way? Yes, the cul-de-sac by the old corner shop. He'll be by the third tree on the left. He's not in a good state. No, no, there's no reason to call an ambulance – he's just drunk. Look, I'll pay extra. Okay. Okay. Okay. Alright.'

Cassandra hangs up, takes out her wallet, and shoves her remaining money into Fox's hands.

'Try and stay awake until the taxi gets here,' she says.

Then Cassandra walks quickly to the campfire and towards the distant groans, the blue light of her mobile extending before her. For a short while, guided by this tiny light, she remains calm, but soon images of all the horrible things that could be happening to Billy begin to creep inside her mind. All around she can see the eyes of the roaches, hear their chattering. She imagines them puncturing Billy's throat with their mandibles, draining his blood, carrying him off to Old Grey to be consumed.

Cassandra begins to run, stumbling over the rocky and uneven forest floor.

Then she slips, trips over the roots of a tree, and lands with a crack on her shoulder.

Lying on her side she gazes up at the moon and wonders why humans are such a pain.

There is another groan – this one so close it sends vibrations up along her spine. She stands up and struggles forward. Up ahead she can just about make out a clearing. As she draws closer it becomes more and more distinct – a moonlit gap in the forest where two shadows stand.

One is a tall and unintelligible dark mass. Sometimes appearing like a giant creature – all fangs and arms. Sometimes just a tree or a hill.

The other is short and, as Cassandra comes to the very edge of the clearing, she sees that it is Billy – but not a Billy she knows. There is something different, a dazed half-full quality to his eyes. She feels a familiar fear welling up in her gut.

The Billy who is not quite Billy, holds up his arms to the other shadow as if to embrace it.

Another foghorn call sounds from the woods.

It is so loud Cassandra can't tell if it is coming from that shape or from elsewhere.

Panicked, she bolts between Billy and the shadow, waving her phone threateningly.

'Go on!' she yells. 'Get out of here!'

In the flicker of her torch, Cassandra thinks she sees glimpses of an exoskeleton, beak-like jaw, translucent wings, long antennae, fibrous hairs.

Then, just as quickly, that impression is gone.

All that is in front of her are trees and tiny roaches' eyes looking at her and her friend like the spying angels of an aloof, uncaring god.

Billy, his arms still outstretched, falls to his knees.

Cassandra glares at him. 'What were you doing out here?' she asks.

Billy does not reply.

'Did you want to die?'

Billy does not reply.

Cassandra feels a sudden urge to thump him.

Then the battery in her mobile whimpers and shuts down, leaving them only with moonlight, starlight and bug-light.

The dark green GOTE painted onto Billy's body blends almost completely into the night.

All Cassandra can see are patches of pale skin and the milky whites of his eyes – puzzle pieces of the person she knows.

'You know,' says Billy, 'I wish my mind was like one of my instruments. That all that was needed was for a few strings to be adjusted, some dials turned, and all my thoughts would chime harmoniously.'

Cassandra doesn't know what to say to that. She doesn't know what to say to any of it – to this fractured shadow. She doesn't know what to say to make all the pieces of Billy come together again.

Before she knows what is happening, her feet are walking.

Walking away from the clearing, deep into the forest.

Dandelion Bug Farm\

Sky Walk

Waiting

Room

'Here we are,' says Simon, bringing the car to a halt. 'This is where almost a third of the GOTE in Goregree is produced. Not much to look at is it? Quite humble.'

'Well, it's a drug production facility in an abandoned shithole town. I would be surprised if it was flashy.'

'Hmm. I guess.'

Alice always finds Simon to be a little clueless when it comes to his work. He talks about it as if it were some quaint homespun business.

The 'farm' consists of a pig pen, a chicken coop, a shack, and a small bungalow. It looks like a child's idea of a farm – the sort of quaint slice of nothing a middle-class couple going through a mid-life crisis might buy. Alice can imagine it being featured on one of those trashy midday property programmes where it would be described with words like 'authentic' and 'rugged'.

'Come,' says Simon. 'I will show you where we make the GOTE. Also, could you pass me a beer?' He starts leading her towards the pig pen.

'Are you certain it's okay for me to be here?'

'Yeaaaah. It'll be fine.'

Simon unlocks the gate and gestures for Alice to follow.

Alice tiptoes in, trying not to spill her beer on any of the snoring pigs who are slumbering disorganised all about the pen, wheezing painfully in their sleep. No doubt all the females have been force-fed roaches during the day.

By the back wall, Simon sweeps aside some hay to uncover a trap door. He pulls it open, revealing a black pit beneath. 'Come take a look,' he says, clambering into the pit.

Alice winces, crouches, then lowers her legs cautiously into the black hole. She shudders as she feels the moist stale air in the space below, bites her lip, then drops down. 'Shaaaah!' she exclaims as her shoes land with a clomp on a smooth stone floor. 'This place is freezing, Simon.'

'Yeah,' he says, fiddling with something by the wall. 'We have to keep it that way. Jars have got to stay cool.'

A light comes on and the black pit is revealed to be some kind of cellar filled with stacks upon stacks of jars each containing an animal foetus suspended in yellow fluid.

'Ugh. This is vile, Simon.'

'Really? I think it's pretty cool,' he says. 'Come take a look over here.' He points to a table with various Bunsen burners and elaborate interconnected test tubes.

'My boss has been experimenting with new preservation fluids. We're wondering if there's not a compound fluid we could try that would retain more potency. Degradation of potency is one of the main technical barriers holding back efficient mass production.'

'Can we just smoke now? These dead animal jars are totally mank.'

There is a grinding of gravel outside. A car pulling up?

'Shit,' says Simon. 'Uhhh, before we smoke, I better go have a word with my boss.'

Alice scowls. 'I thought you said me being here wouldn't be a problem.'

'And it isn't. I just need to go have a word with him beforehand. Could you wait down here for a bit?'

'With the creepy animal foetuses?'

He nods, hands cupped in a pleading gesture.

Alice rolls her eyes. 'Be quick about it.'

'Thanks.' Simon grabs a fold-up little ladder from under the desk. 'Back in a minute,' he says, as he climbs out.

Alice sits on a wooden stool by the desk.

Then she waits.

And waits.

And waits.

Christ, how long has he been gone? She checks her phone. Only five minutes? It feels like forever.

Stuff this, she thinks. Diving up the ladder, she sneaks back to the car. Checking the door, she is glad to see it is still unlocked. After a minute of rummaging around in the dark, she finds a bag of GOTE under the seat. Quickly pulling out a bag of rollies, she assembles a vaguely smokable cylinder. She can't quite call it a spliff.

It is only after she's left the car, lit up, and sucked in that first mouthful of black smoke, that it occurs to Alice that the GOTE bag under the seat of the car might be uncut.

Suddenly she feels every cell in her body, every pore in her skin, opening, closing; the electricity running through her hairs, the ground beneath her feet, every contour of the rock and the soil. She reaches out her hand. Feels the wind. The wind gliding round the edge of her fingers. The grooves in her fingerprints like rings in the core of an oak tree. The grooves in her brain like the rings in the core of an oak tree. Her brain like an oak tree split. Her brain warm like the core of the Earth. The core of the Earth like her hot heart beating, beating, beating.

Alice is in a field of dandelions, grass, and mud.

How has she got here?

When did she get naked?

No matter.

She lies on her back looking up at the purple, early morning sky. Feels the softness of cold wet grass beneath her back. Feels the softness of dandelion fluff-seeds beneath her nails. Feels the softness of squelchy earth squishing into her scalp.

In the distance she can hear two men arguing.

'Are you fucking mental? This is our place of work. What the hell are you thinking bringing a customer back here?'

'Hey. Alice is an old friend. She's not just a customer.'

'I don't care who the daft junkie slag is. What the fuck are we going to do if she ODs or something? Get her the fuck out of here.'

The rest descends into an unintelligible murk – even though Alice feels like her hearing is sharper than it has ever been. It is just that words don't make sense any more. They are animal noises. No different from birds or crickets chirping.

Alice thinks about an article she read online about an experiment in which mice were exposed to drugs. At first the mice were only given drugs in total isolation. Very soon they all became addicted and neurotic. Then the scientists tried again but this time they gave the mice toys, good food, space to roam, and let them hang out together rather than live in isolation. Almost none of the mice became addicted. The person writing the article said that the experiment showed that drug addiction was a societal problem – that if we structured society well then addiction would be minimised.

Thinking about it now, Alice comes to a different conclusion. 'Almost none' means some. And that means that even in a hypothetically perfect society some people will still be on junk.

A part of her also wonders if it isn't all junk. Who is to say that toys, property, stimulating conversation, fucking and good food aren't all in their own way just junk?

Another part of her is sad. She imagines those little mice hitting the button on their little cocaine drip. Hammering the 'I'm Alive' button as hard they can until they just don't have the strength any more. She imagines their soft white fur beneath her fingertips. Her fingerprints like rings on a tree. And so on.

Alice feels her spirit soaring upward, leaving her body on the cold grass.

Upward and upward, until it shoots through the blue-black blanket of night.

Upward and upward, until everything is dark and silent.

Then, all of a sudden, Alice finds herself in a white room, in a white chair.

It looks like a waiting room in a hospital but something tells Alice that it is not a normal waiting room. Nonetheless, it feels familiar. Very familiar. There are five seats in the room, one of which she is sitting on, another of which seems to be occupied by a young man. No. Not quite. At least not yet. More like the shadow of one. A hazy silhouette. Regardless, something tells her she knows the person this shadow belongs to and that it will not be long before he joins her. In fact, as she casts her eyes to the other three chairs, she feels a twinge of recognition. She thinks she catches in those chairs glimpses of dark familiar things waiting to become solid.

Alice feels odd, serene like never before.

Above her a clock ticks.

She folds her arms and waits.

Places For People\ People\ The Last Storm of Mr Jones

'Rough day, man?' asks the taxi driver, ten minutes into the journey.

Louie opens his mouth to answer but nothing comes out. His mouth hangs gaping for a moment then shuts.

'That bad?' says the driver, his expression shadowed by a broad-beaked baseball cap, a red and white thing with the word 'Player' emblazoned in gold. Louie wonders how he can see from under there.

'You smell of pussy,' the man continues. 'Can't have been that bad an evening if you come home smelling of pussy.'

Louie gives him a stern look.

'Hey. Don't be weird about it. I'm just yanking your chain.' He extends a hairy finger and pokes a bauble hanging from the rear view mirror, a playing card with a naked woman on it and some words beneath that Louie can't read in the dark. 'This here is what you need. All you need in life is pussy, weed, and cash. Got that?'

Louie stares for a moment at the drab bit of cardboard depicting a woman – no, only the idea of a woman – and thinks for a brief second that maybe the driver has suggested something profound. Then a smell wafts up from below.

'Sorry. That was me,' says the driver. 'Anyway, we're nearly there. Just around this corner, isn't it? I tell you, I've been living in this shithole for ages and I still can barely find my way around these rabbit-warren streets. Why don't you Brits try building places for people?'

'I have no idea. I'm not from around here.'

'Yeah. Heard that one. No one ever is.'

The taxi halts outside the Jones' shop.

Louie reaches into his wallet and hands the driver £20.

'Really? Haven't got that much change, man.'

'No. Take the whole lot. Doesn't matter.'

'That's quite the tip. You sure you don't—'

Louie steps out of the car before the man can finish. He is tired of talking to people. It's exhausting. The repetitious anti-climactic cycle of it. The moment just before the other person talks when anticipation is highest. The expectation. The hope that they might say something different and surprising. The sinking disappointment when they don't. And then the hollow, aching disappointment when you don't either.

As Louie turns the key in the lock and opens the door to the shop, he wonders if humans are no different than animals barking the same calls to each other over and over until extinction. He steps inside and breathes in the air of the shop – dusty boxes and rotting stock. Then he goes upstairs to have a shower. As he steps into the bathroom and strips off his clothes, Louie groans. There is a dead roach the size of a tennis ball laying on its back over the plug. Picking up a shampoo bottle he smashes it until it slides down through the grating in bits, like rice being forced through a sieve. Then he goes to the shower nozzle, angles it away from his body, and cranks the faucet. He sits down on the floor and lets the warm spray blast to the side of him, remaining mostly cool and dry, being hit only indirectly by small droplets.

Louie has been doing this since he was six. Done right, he'd found that it would cause pleasant tingles to shiver along the surface of his skin making his hairs stand on end as if electrified. As a child he would sit in the corner of the shower with the shampoo and conditioner bottles. He would pretend that the shower was a tremendous downpour and that he was a homeless person huddled under a roof which barely sheltered him. The shampoo and conditioner were his fellow homeless friends. Louie invented back stories and personalities for them. Together they would huddle for warmth and tell tales to each other around an imaginary bin with a fire in it.

Eventually, when the time came for Louie to actually engage with the business of washing, he would pretend that he had to leave, that the roof wasn't big enough to shelter all of them, that he had to sacrifice himself for the good of the group. Then he would walk out into the rain. The shampoo and conditioner would cry – *don't go*. But he would dissolve before them like dirt in water.

Now, with his mother gone, his father nearly dead from drink, the family business falling to pieces around his isolated, hopelessly-out-of-its-depth nineteen-year-old head, Louie finds that childhood make-believe game strangely prescient. Maybe even then he was wishing he could die in a way that would make everything right.

Ten minutes pass. No pleasant sensation comes. Maybe he isn't doing the trick right?

Oh well. No matter. He splashes a bit of water on himself, turns off the shower and reaches for his towel. Then he realises he's forgotten to bring a change of clothes.

Fuck it, he thinks. No matter. No matter. It doesn't matter. Not where I'm going, going, going, gone, gone, go...

Louie realises he is down the hallway now. Naked. Dick swaying in the stale store air.

He sees his hand knocking on the door to his father's room. The last time he'd done this he'd got a smack for his trouble. 'You still alive in there, cunt?' he shouts.

Louie shoves open the door and is assaulted by the smell of excrement and booze. All over the floor, from the doorway to the foot of his father's bed, are vodka bottles, lager cans, wine bottles – some empty, some half-full, some filled with piss. He hears a whisper from beneath soiled sheets.

'Lou?'

'So you are still alive, I take it?'

'Lou, come here.'

Louie tiptoes around the glasses, but it is hard to make out everything in the gloom and it isn't long before he knocks over a pint glass full of vomit.

'Blast,' he mutters.

'Closer,' says his father, 'I want to have a look at you.'

'Why? Are you going to finally come downstairs?'

'Just come closer.'

Louie edges a little closer. Suddenly a hand reaches out from under the blankets. Louie flinches, thinking his father might hit him again like six weeks prior. But when he sees his withered hand – his frail, shaking hand too weak to even form a fist – he feels stupid for even thinking that.

'Ha,' says his dad, 'pull my finger.'

Louie looks at him, confused.

'Come on now. Don't leave me hanging.'

Louie grabs his father's finger. It feels like a twig that might snap at the slightest exertion.

'I remember,' his dad rasps, 'when your little finger could barely wrap round mine. It was so small.'

Louie can't see his father's face but can sense him smiling somewhere in the filth-covered blankets.

'I promise,' the old man says, 'I promise I will come down tomorrow. Tell your mother not to worry. This will be the last storm of mine.'

The same, Louie thinks. The same grunts and calls, over and over, until you just want it all to stop. He closes his eyes. He can't bear to look at him any more. He stumbles back over the bottles to the doorway.

'I love you, son.'

Louie wants more than anything to turn around and say, 'I know. That's why it hurts.' Instead he just says 'I...' and his mouth hangs open for a painful minute.

He goes downstairs to the shop floor. The dusty tiles are cool beneath his bare feet. He strides over to a window and cracks it open, breathes in fresh oxygen, feels it curve and flow around his naked body. Of course, it only seems fresh comparatively. Intellectually Louie knows that this close to the woods every mouthful of air is filled with tiny poisonous bug fragments. But regardless, something deep within, something instinctual, buried in the nerve endings and neurons of his spine, wants to believe the air is fresh. That he has a choice. That he is making a decision.

He begins to laugh.

Climbing on top of the store counter, like he'd done as a child, like he'd got yelled at for doing by his dad, the young man reaches up towards the rifle on the display.

Dirty Vessels\
A Light Goes Out

Humans are nothing but dirty water.

This idea comes to Cassandra as she staggers over the twigs and roots of the forest, feeling round rocks beneath the soles of her space boots pushing up into the arches of her feet. Though perhaps the groundwork for the idea's emergence was laid many years before when she watched *They Came From Alpha Centauri* – for it was then that Cassandra first made the connection between people and water.

Water is the clearest expression of purity in the universe – giver of life, taker of nothing, always changing yet always itself, transparent, clear, without secrets.

The people of Alpha Centauri are a hundred percent waterabsolute perfection.

The people of Earth meanwhile are only seventy-five percent. Close but not quite. Opaque. Clouded with bad chemicals and bad ideas. You can't read them clearly.

Cassandra wonders whether she too has become opaque – whether being on this planet has polluted her. Maybe that is why her people haven't come to save her yet? No, no, no, no. She must not think like that. Not like that.

Something buzzes past her visor and interrupts her absent-minded march.

Standing still for a moment, Cassandra can see the firefly eyes of the roaches piercing through the black foliage. Their tiny clicking voices sound like distant chimes. Their delicate wings shimmer in the early morning light like shards of blue glass. So pretty. Yet every flutter sends a puff of poison out into the night.

One light seems out of place, though, amongst the

insect eyes. It hangs higher in the air than the others. The way it flickers seems more artificial, mechanical. Cassandra finds herself heading towards it. She wonders if this is wise. There are all sorts of human stories of eerie lights luring people to their doom. Will-o'-the-wisps that mesmerise and lure you into bogs, leaving you to drown in muddy pools. Lanterns set on seaside cliffs to deceive passing ships, leading them to crash against rocks. These fearful thoughts do not cause Cassandra's feet to stop moving though – they have long since ceased to take orders from her.

As she draws closer, the distant light takes on a more recognisable shape.

It is a street lamp but by no street Cassandra can recognise.

All around, nestled amongst the foliage, are vine-covered fibreglass domes each the size of a small shed. Snaking between the structures is the faint outline of what looks to have been a footpath. Cassandra steps on to it hesitantly as if it might disappear. Following the trail, she can just about make out through the dense weeds and grasses, little placards that are mostly illegible and propped on rusty metal stands.

Reaching the street lamp, standing beneath its modest light, Cassandra wonders what this place once was. Perhaps some sort of arboretum or garden? Whatever it was it has long since been surrendered to the forest. The domes look like desiccated fruit, husks that might disintegrate at any moment.

The only thing that suggests otherwise is the little lonely lamp flickering stubbornly in the dark. It is not eerie at all now. Cassandra finds herself reaching out towards to it, feeling she might hold it, hug it, champion this mundane source of brightness.

Then, with a *zzzt*, the lamp goes out and she is in the dark again, feeling foolish and sad.

She wonders why she has run into the woods, why she's stayed out so late, why she came out at all? Why not lay in the bath like her mum did and wait for rescue? Does part of her not believe? Does part of her not want to let go of this dirty world and its dirty people? Is it simply a revolt of her human vessel. Or is it something more?

She presses onwards past the forgotten domes and back into the roach-filled woods. Their voices seem less musical now. Rather they are high-pitched and irritating, like laughter. She is so tired. How long has she been walking? Where is she?

Then, as she ascends a slight slope, a break in the trees appears up ahead. She is right by the Jones' corner shop – a short walk from home. And, though the door is shut, the lights are still on downstairs so it can't be that late either. There is a good chance that the Lunar Window is still open. Relieved, she gallops down the ridge to the road that divides the woods and the housing estate. But, as she steps onto the tarmac, she hears raised voices coming from the shop, voices which grow louder and louder into a series of shouts she can't make out through the muffling of concrete and glass.

Then there is a bang. A bang louder than anything Cassandra has ever heard. A bang that sucks all sound out from the world. She stands in the middle of the road, frozen like earlier that day. In the window of the shop she sees a shadow holding what looks like a gun. She can't tell if it is Louie or his father. She doesn't know which possibility frightens her more.

The lights in the shop go out.

For a few minutes Cassandra is paralysed in the middle of the road – looking at her orange space boots and the road beneath them. Then she crosses over to the pavement and continues walking. She decides she's seen nothing. That her mind is playing tricks, polluted after a bad evening. Besides, something like that couldn't happen. Shouldn't happen. Did it happen? It didn't happen.

As she turns the corner onto her street, Cassandra feels incredibly cold. By the time she gets to her front door her gloved hands are shaking. Once inside she scrapes the forest mud off her space boots and goes through to the living room to check that Fox has made it in okay. He is there, asleep, dirty, near-naked, breathing faintly on her lemon-green sofa.

Leaving the lights off, she takes out her phone and tiptoes to the table where her charger is. She wants to check the time, make sure she hasn't missed the Lunar Window. There is a beep as she plugs in her mobile, followed by a whirring vibration as a text comes in. It is from Billy:

I'm sorry

Cassandra isn't certain if he is apologising for his actions tonight or for some future grievance. Isn't 'I'm sorry' the sort of thing people say before they do something terrible and stupid? Cassandra feels exhausted just thinking about it. How is it possible for two words to contain so many bad ideas?

There is a sigh like trapped air escaping a cadaver. Fox's eyes half open.

'Hey, Cass,' he whispers in a frail voice.

'Sorry,' says Cassandra. 'I didn't mean to wake you.'

'It's no worry,' he says. 'Is Billy okay?'

'I don't know,' she says, sitting on the arm of the sofa, looking blankly into nothing.

'Oh. Alright. I guess it's hard to know really.' In the early morning gloom Fox seems a thousand years old – like an ancient statue that might turn to dust at the slightest prod.

'Will you be going home tonight?' he asks. 'I mean, your real home.'

'I hope so,' replies Cassandra, 'I have a good feeling.'

'That's nice,' he says. 'Could I come with you?'

'I don't think so,' she says. 'I don't think humans can live on Alpha Centauri.'

'Well,' he says, 'we're not doing such a good job living here either.' Fox begins to laugh but his squawking goosey giggle is quickly throttled into a rasping cough. 'So tell me, Cass, what's Alpha Centauri like?'

'It's an orb of calm water orbiting an emerald star. There are no clouds. The dawn is crisp and clear.'

'Sounds gorgeous.' And with that Fox's eyes draw shut and he becomes still – stiller than Cassandra has ever seen him before.

She checks the time on her charging mobile: 03:00. Later than she would like but still within the parameters. As she tiptoes out of the living room and into the hallway, her eyes are drawn to a lone picture hanging on the wall by the staircase – a photo of her at GCSE graduation with her fifth, and last, foster carer, a large woman named Sally who was perpetually smoking and out of the house. As she walks past and up the stairs, Cassandra barely recognises the little girl depicted. The baggy uniform and long blonde hair seem so alien. Only the detached expression feels familiar – an unbroken line of continuity.

Stepping into the bathroom, boots plodding on the chequered tiles, she flicks on the light switch and finally sees the full state of herself reflected in the mirror. Her orange spacesuit is covered in dirt and grime and blood. Thankfully there are no tears in the material or cracks in the visor. Wetting a cloth, she sets about wiping the suit clean of all the gunge and grot. And, as she does this, Cassandra feels the events of the evening slipping into the back of her mind. Her attention turns fully to her journey to the stars. She wants to be presentable. She wants her parents to find a woman just as clean as the girl they'd left. A person undirtied by bad chemicals or bad ideas. A vessel that is transparent and clear.

Satisfied, she climbs into the bath while still in her spacesuit and turns on the tap. Then she lays down on her back and lets the water flow around her, creep around the sides of her visor. Cassandra imagines herself in one of the underwater cities gazing out at the vast oceanic utopia of Alpha Centauri. She looks up at the ceiling and thinks of the spaceship floating above – her mother and the father she's never met, waiting on board.

Her face strains and cracks into a smile as wide and white as a crescent moon.

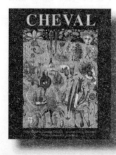

Praise for *Bad Ideas\Chemicals*

'*Bad Ideas\Chemicals* is set in the fictional town of Goregree. Here, its 20s-something denizens face down a future of dope, dishevelment, and disenfranchisement, mostly on a bad night, and usually among the town's clubs and bars. Lloyd Markham channels William Burroughs filtered through William Gibson and adds a touch of Iain Sinclair's trek among the abandoned mental hospitals of the M25 ring. The result is a dark-humoured mix of post-Goth trainwreck, gyppo vamp and hipster slutism. It sits well in a world where the best job on offer is working at the local privatised euthanasia clinic and the drug of choice is GOTE, a much sought after compound derived from crushed insects and pregnant animals. When not confounded by parents from Alpha Centauri or women at the corner shop who know his foster carers our author hero lives a life permanently compromised by cheap booze, failed sex and bad chemicals. Among the housing estates, dark wet roads, bus shelters and street lamps does anything really happen? Probably not, but that certainly shouldn't stop you reading.'

PETER FINCH

'A dark and witty take on small town life, where nothing is normal no matter how familiar it might seem. This is a story of misfits, of haunted twenty-somethings and their struggle to move on from the mess of their teenage years. That struggle has rarely felt so essential, so raw, or as powerful as it does in this debut.'

DAVID TOWSEY

'Dark, bleak, weird, grim, cool ... it will probably become a cult classic.'

RHIAN ELIZABETH

'Poignant, unnervingly funny and poetic, *Bad Ideas\Chemicals* puts us inside lives lived on the edge of nowhere, like an old-time Frost Fair, dancing on thin ice above dark waters of the real desperation of our times.'

PHILIP GROSS

'The desolation of *The Man who Fell to Earth* and the pathos of *Stand by Me*, with the nakedness and immediacy of *In and out of The Goldfish Bowl*. Contains single sentences written with such brevity and diffidence they deserve covers of their own.'

M.A.OLIVER-SEMENOV

'Imagine the latter day offspring of a threesome between Caradoc Evans, Sherwood Anderson and a Larson cartoon. The result might be *Bad Ideas\Chemicals*. Markham's town of Goregree isn't quite dystopia, or satire, or magic realism. Perhaps it's dirty dystopic unmagic nonrealism. It's as messy and intriguing as it sounds, portraying an inimical, bug-infested world in which everything is both ordinary and strange and in which no one feels as if they belong. Always at its heart is a sense of outraged humaneness. Some writers try to do weird. Some writers do weird. Lloyd Markham is weird.'

CHRISTOPHER MEREDITH

'Part *Clockwork Orange*, part *Brave New World, Bad Ideas\ Chemicals* is wholly its own entity. Brimming with dark ideas and philosophies in a nightmarish post-Brexit world, it is the humanity of the central characters that pulls you through the darkness to the bittersweet conclusion. This series of intricately crafted vignettes marks Lloyd Markham as a unique new voice.'

RHYS THOMAS